Other work by the author:

Soul Resin (2002)
Katrina Means Cleansing (2015)
French Quarter Beautification Project (2016)

SLEEPYTIME DOWN SOUTH

C. W. CANNON

Livingston Press
The University of West Alabama

Copyright © 2017 C. W. Cannon
All rights reserved, including electronic text

ISBN 13: 978-1-60489-198-0, trade paper
ISBN 13: 978-1-60489-199-7, hardcover
ISBN: 1-60489-198-X, trade paper
ISBN: 1-60489-199-8, hardcover
Library of Congress Control Number 2017948800
Printed on acid-free paper
by Publishers Graphics
Printed in the United States of America

Hardcover binding by: Heckman Bindery
Typesetting and page layout: Joe Taylor, Teresa Boykin
Proofreading: Shelby Parrish, Erin Watt, Teresa Boykin
Cover design: Teresa Boykin

Cover photo: C. W. Cannon
Photo of author: Demaris Anderson

This is a work of fiction:
any resemblance
to persons living or dead is coincidental.

Livingston Press is part of The University of West Alabama,
and thereby has non-profit status.
Donations are tax-deductible:
brothers and sisters, we need 'em.

First edition
6 5 4 3 3 2 1

SLEEPYTIME DOWN SOUTH

"The observations and comings-and-goings of a solitary and quiet, serious-minded person are murkier, yet more urgent than those of the socialite. His thoughts are heavier, perhaps more magical, yet never without a sad streak. Mundane images and perceptions that most would glibly dismiss with a glance and a laugh, with an easy rationalization, trouble him unduly; he steeps them in silence until they assume meanings, become Experience, Adventure, Feeling. Loneliness occasions originality, daring and disarming beauty—the Poem. But loneliness also occasions the inverse, what is disproportionate, absurd, forbidden."

Thomas Mann, "Death in Venice"
(Translation C. W. C.)

SIDE A

I. DETOUR AHEAD 🎺 SLOW♪

Smooth road, clear day,
But why am I the only one traveling this way?
How strange the road to love should be so
Easy…
—as sung by Sarah Vaughan,
March 7, 1958 at Chicago's *London House*

Peter "Maz" Mazewski was once dubbed "the Benny Goodman of his generation." In one of the *Playboy* jazz polls. Probably '62, '63. But the moniker turned him against the clarinet. He drifted over to alto sax, where he found a new home, new fans, new sound. He got nominated for a Grammy, and after his 1972 fusion soft funk break-out, *Preaching the Blues*, people started calling him "Reverend" Maz.

One October afternoon in 1982 he woke up in a funk. Not the good kind. A bad blue funk, without groove. He knew before he got out of bed that he had to quit his sweet home, Chicago. And he knew before he left the house that it would have to be New Orleans. Follow the funk to the crotch and find out—that was his plan.

He made a few phone calls. Put off his producer, said you can't rush art. Then he hit the pavement with a light bag and a not too special *Selmer*. Union Station was step one, the first crossroads, where he'd pick a gate that led to another one, and on and on till he found his baby. He dug Union Station deeply, always had. Decked out like it knew how monumental it was, flinging passengers to the far corners like lightning bolts, or dust.

But only about thirty lonely souls is what Maz counted in the vestibule. The big black pews looked so empty. What happened to the crowds? History. Maz used to make it a point to show up early, just to love the bustle, all the bodies and suits and hats and faces, standing, sitting, strutting, passed out, tearing out running. He wanted to hear Strayhorn's *A-train*, or 'Trane's blue one, a fighting blue. But all that came to him was *Detour Ahead*. Dogged by that itch again, which seemed to just be saying lay down and die. No way *if the blues don't leave me ... rock on away from there.*

He hopped aboard the Illinois Central. Well, now it was Amtrak. "The City of New Orleans." He wondered if it was the only line still surviving named after a city. It was a no-brainer that it would be the grimiest train in the Amtrak inventory. A cinch, since it had to traverse Mississippi and grind to a halt in the Big Greasy. His coach car was a hand-me-down for sure. With its faded walls from the glory days, out in the sunny blue west: dulled Formica thunderbirds in red and blue, on a golden yellow background.

Inappropriate attire. Embarrassing. Maybe for what they did out west these birds got banished to the south, to America's own little hell. Or was it America's secret playground, an all-too earthly paradise?

But the decor didn't matter, it was more the people, the

train-goers, that Maz was into. He could afford a berth, but he always rode coach. To see the people, the people who rode the train, getting on, getting off. The little things they said, the way they said them, the looks on their faces. Different threads, hairdos. Different colors. His favorite poet said *I am a colossus, I contain multitudes* (something like that), and that was the way Maz went about things when he got down. It was about seeing America, feeling it, the people. Joining the throng. He wanted to figure them all out, even though he knew you never could. Maybe love them.

What made Maz different from the others (as far as he knew) was that he didn't know where to get off. Hadn't decided yet. He booked passage to the end of the line, but didn't think he'd go all the way down. New Orleans was just too much. He just wanted to relax and soak up some country Americans. The plan was to jump off in Mississippi somewhere. Smell out some country blues. Maybe Memphis.

But Chi was still very much around, still chugging on by, a whole hour since boarding. From brick warehouse to brick bungalow to brick warehouse again, repeat, repeat. But finally they hit the amber waves, the endless horizon of cultivated field that never let up for the three-hundred miles of Illinois. The crush of the city gone, he could finally sleep.

Soundly. His car swayed like a crib.

He woke up only when the gray dawn happened around Memphis. He pried his peepers open, and shut them and opened them again. He knew it was Memphis. Definitely city brick. Again. And enough of it to be a city. But why did this southern brick look different than Chicago's? His eyes closed again and his dreams chewed over strange theories on the brick and other issues. Something about flesh, boiled in a big pot out on the grass, going into the southern brick and making it more malleable. But then his lids flapped up again and the dream was gone and there was the live brick again. Still Memphis. Still the same two brick corners framing the same unvehicled road, under the train on the same old trestle, same bolted steel crossbeam from dreams and dreams ago.

But the bridge was as good as any to be stuck on, the road a random American road.

Not bad. Could be Chi—drawn to smaller scale, of course. And more bruised, broken, more beaten by foliage. Chicago had blight—but this wasn't blight. This was a lackadaisical attitude toward upkeep. The tracks had debris thrown on them, an old mattress, a tire, and no one bothered to tidy their work space. Lazy turkey-neck land. So quick to discard something if it requires the least effort.

The South. He hated it. What was he doing here? This southern indolence thing had a vicious streak to it. It was disrespecting of other folks' labor to let perfectly sound structures go to hell. To request that maybe the living should get up and work would be a glove-throwable offense. Predictably, the train also refused to work. It was some other train's job to move the customers down the track.

Maz fumed until he saw something move. Not the train, though: some living thing, down in the junk on the unused—

one hoped—tracks. It was a hand reaching out of a crate. It retreated. It re-appeared. A black hand, palm down on the rail bed gravel. It was somebody's home out there on the train tracks. A Byzantine row, in the rough shape of a crescent, of cardboard boxes, some wooden ones, plywood, blankets, sheeted plastic. Vernacular palace. Overstuffed garbage bags lying around like sacks of tribute. The hand had grown into a torso, on elbows and knees, emerging from the enclosure. It stood.

A man. He was wrapped in two, maybe three bathrobes, in clashing colors and patterns. He was black. And old. Matted gray beard with weeds, grass in it. The rest of the face was unseen under an ultra-wide straw brim, like a sombrero. When he stooped, to dig around in a garbage bag, Maz saw also a red bandanna peeking out from under the hat in back. The rail bed satrap rose again with an old coffee can and a wire coat hanger. He turned to face Maz's coach and raised his head. The face was wide and dark, framed by grizzled gray fuzz. The mouth spread slowly into a warm smile. At Maz? Could he see him? The man raised up an arm and waved the coat hanger. At Maz? An invitation?

Maz scanned the faces he could see in the coach car. They all slept. He looked out again and saw the old chief was beating out a rhythm on the coffee can, holding up his head and pointing his eyes the same way the train was pointing, intoning something. Maz couldn't hear it. The train lurched into gear. Labored forward and the weird messenger turned and looked full at where he must have known Maz to be.

The train didn't get a whole lot farther before winding down again. This time Maz jumped up and patted his pockets and ran a hand through his hair and said "excuse me" to nobody in particular. "Um, this is my stop. I'm getting off here."

A few eyes opened and closed again and some bodies shifted around in their chairs. But all in all, Maz was ignored. The train was still stationary, though, so Maz grabbed his bag from up top and his alto from under the seat and beat it for the exit.

But he was stopped by a porter. A middle aged brown man with a bureaucratic paunch, indignation planted all over his mug. He said, "Excuse me." With finality.

Maz said it too, and added, "But this is my stop. I need to get off here."

"We done left the station."

"But it's right out there!"

"What?"

"Memphis," Maz said, and pointed at the window.

The porter laughed, with too much glee. "That's Clarksdale. We done left Memphis. Hour ago."

Maz was puzzled. Clarksdale? "I didn't even know this train stopped at Clarksdale."

"Well, no," the porter admitted. "Not usually. We had to take a detour. Tallahatchie bridge got flooded out."

Maz hadn't seen any rain.

"Gotta wait for Yazoo."

The porter escorted Maz back to his place. Then he glimmed Maz' reservation stub and his eyelids tightened into a righteous squint, the kind that goes with "Pshaw!" in the comic books. He chuckled. "Well, you bound for New Orleans. You got a ways to go yet."

"I know, I just did that."

"Did what?"

"Nothing."

"You got family on board?"

Now Maz felt dipped in shame, but didn't know why he should. "Yeah, yeah," he muttered, and took his seat. The porter let him alone. Maz knew he didn't really look old enough for senile. He had his hair still. It was all white but had been from way back. He silvered early. He was trim, fit. He'd never been not trim, in fact, in his whole life. No matter how much he ate or drank, he never could add much flesh to his bony frame. He preferred to think of himself as lithe (as opposed to skinny). But he wasn't putting the energy into dud selection that he once did. He most of the time wore exactly what he wore now—jeans and a dark sweatshirt. He blamed society: if nobody else went to the trouble anymore of suiting up for a train trip, he wasn't going to hassle with it, either.

He sat in his assigned seat feeling peeved, not wanting to look at anyone, eyes trained on the outside, the flip-side of the scratched Plexiglas. At least they were moving again.

He felt like crying. Happened all the time lately. Tears backing up, trying to bust out, but he never let them. That'd be like giving up. Because he couldn't think up a legitimate reason why he should. He didn't do anything, and nobody did anything *to* him, to merit a weepy fit. Too many people let their emotions lead them around on a chain. It wasn't that they were weak, but these over-hormoned cases treated the blind, dumb wellings of the psyche as some kind of external force over which they had no control. Maz treated his rainy moods like spoiled children. They needed to be dealt with firmly, or else they'd take over and run your whole life into a big sobbing mess. If you did that, you were half a foot away from going junkie and domming in an alley. It might be painful, but, please, be the master of your own house. People made the same mistake in art, in music, too. Just shouted out their spleens or their balls or some other fatty tissue. All that pop psycho-babble about "repression" was just an excuse to never grow up.

    Maz disembarked at Rolling Fork. In search of glory days. Freedom summers. Across the street from the station was the business row. Now mostly shuttered. Some of the awnings over the sidewalk sagged enough that Maz thought it safest to walk around them. He was headed to a place he remembered from before, the Glenburnie Motor Lodge. Looked like the Bates Motel, but in town and with a brightly lit twenty-four hour restaurant. Used to be a good place to line your flue for cheap. Across the street was once the dingy office with the acronym on the door, where Maz and a carload of Chicago friends once loaded up on coffee and clipboards, pencils, and "literature." Before fanning out into enemy and victim territory. The structure remained, Maz was happy to see. But the office seemed now to be a mortuary chapel. They'd put white-washed plywood over the big picture window. Hand-painted black letters said, "Tilly's Funeral Services." On the door they'd painted a cross. They'd also stuck a white-painted iron cross up on the flat roof.

The Glenburnie restaurant hadn't changed much. Not even the leathery breakfast ham that Maz couldn't get through in 'sixty-four, either. But the society working and eating there was definitely arranged differently. His waitress was black, but another section had a white waitress serving a party of black men. The counter was evenly mixed, and in many cases the same feed company caps sat on heads of different shades who sat and ate and laughed and apparently worked together. It was a vision of integration that Maz rarely (ever?) saw in Chicago. But the whole thing seemed a lot less surprising to the regular patrons than it seemed to Maz. The whole movement back then appeared to Maz suddenly as a big stupid joke on him. Yet he refused to believe that everything was aright in Mississippi. It could never be. The force of history was too great. What was going on here was some kind of blackface lie. Where was the bloody underbelly? Maz felt like provoking something, to see if the façade would hold up under stress, like if he called somebody a 'nigger' or a 'cracker' or something.

But then he recoiled in shock at the notion. What was wrong with him? He'd planned to meet and talk to folks, to find some honky-tonk and mingle with the Mississippians. He was going to take along his axe and blow some blues with the natives. But he knew now he couldn't do that. He was too angry, even if he wasn't sure why. So he took a room, left the horn in the box, and vegetated in front of the tube, trying to pretend he wasn't in the South.

The next morning found him where he knew he'd have to end up all along. He walked back through the gate and re-boarded the "City of New Orleans," this time committed to riding it out, to the end of the line.

He sat in the lounge car and put back scotch and sodas. He figured it was an excellent time to take up smoking again, but when he tried to buy a pack they told him there would be no more smoking on America's transcontinental trains. He made a little scene over it, said, "What the hell's the country coming to if you can't smoke a cigarette on a train to Goddamned New Orleans?"

He looked around him and saw what it was coming to: three cute little family sets with squirming tykes and non-alcoholic beverages. Back in the old days, you could at least find a party in the Jim Crow car. Then he wondered: everybody in the car was white (even the bartender—that is, counter-person). *Was* there in fact a secret car where the blacks congregated, or the men?

A black party did finally show up. And it *was* a party, enough of a party, in fact, to scare off the white family ensembles. The staccato flurry of their voices had preceded them—like an approaching processional. He just listened—

he didn't want to crane around in his seat and gun them with a long stare. It was a group of about four or five, young, all men. They rolled in on loud guffaws and hand-slapping. Lobbing loaded words at each other, like "nigga" and "blood" and "bruh." Wearing gym suits, mostly, and jewelry. Except one, who sat with his back to Maz, with a dress suit, of all things, and a straw hat, fancy type. They were playing some kind of card game where they hurled their cards at the table and dissed their opponents—and their opponents' families—with obscene zeal. But something didn't quite fit in the scene. Maz followed the itch in his mind and got up, picked a timetable off the counter, and re-located to a spot with a wider view. Yes, how strange: they weren't all black. The loudest and wildest of the bunch, in fact, was not black. And not a youth, either. But just as quick to refer to the "black ass" of a rib-ee. He even tossed out the N-word as thoughtlessly as the others.

Maz didn't have to think it over long to realize he was disgusted by this spectacle. The white man was at least thirty years older than the others, and his fashion statement said he had no intention to be considered, mistaken for, one of them. The wide brim Panama hat with a wine-colored band and a cream linen suit (or was it yellow?). And a loud pink tie. And a neatly trimmed, doted-over Faulkner moustache. Why the Old South paternalist look? Parody? Self-parody? If so, his clowning was in poor taste. Strangest thing about him, though, was his accent. Maz tested it by turning away his eyes and turning on his ears. Yep, they all sounded black. White Mississippians didn't talk like this. Chicago white kids—back in the day and probably still—went black and dished the jive, the right words, but never quite got the accent right. Mezzrow was the first cat from Maz' old neighborhood to go black, but he never convinced Maz, either. Jack Teagarden, though, he had the knack. Not with the vocab, so much, just with tone, inflection, accent. And there was that story, if it was true, about Fletcher Henderson taking Teagarden aside at the *Roseland*, saying, "You can trust me, brother—are you passing for white?"

The jawing on the train wended around to where it often did even back in Maz's youth.

"Say, dawg," one of them said, "when you gon' gimme some o'dat sweet?"

"He want dat sweet-sweet," another one chuckled.

Sex or drugs. Did it matter which? Not to an academic observer like Maz.

The white fop, apparently, was in possession of said "sweet-sweet." His face, ruddy, lined, red, was set in a condescending smirk. His wild bright eyes were blue, ice-blue. But what was funny, no, what was "black" about it, was how he used this smirk like it was language, an utterance. He left it hanging out there and waited for a response. The response was laughter all around at the one who wanted the "sweet" (whatever it was). "Aw, Blue, aw, dawg," they guffawed, and reached hands out to Blue, to each other, and finally to the white man, who said, "You too young, Blue. You got to get some hair on yo' balls 'fore you come axin' for dat sweet." Then he lowered his voice, Maz couldn't hear, but it made the other ones bust out laughing again. Something about "spanking" Blue's "black ass?" Was that possible? How could he get away with it? Didn't these guys realize the man was white?

Then the brazen white elder pulled a cigarette out of a silver case and lit it up with a slim shiny lighter and nobody said a damn thing.

Maz got up to re-locate once again. He didn't want to witness this scene any more than he already had. By now the party had sprawled out so much into the corridor, effectively seizing the public space, that Maz had to request permission to get by. He said "excuse me," eyes downcast. A couple of them said, "excuse," and pulled in their legs. But the elder white man took the opportunity to gun Maz hard. Rude. Like some kind of challenge. Maz made it down to the far end of the car but he was trembling from some weird sensation he hadn't felt in…had he ever felt it? Heart racing, hands a-tremble. Then he noticed he was carrying his alto case. This settled him down. Probably the man just saw the case and was just curious. People forgot their manners sometimes, got curious as kittens, over men carrying horns. Maz was just on edge. Wound up tight. But why? What was his problem?

He was shocked at himself, actually, as soon as his analytical penchant caught up with him—it was never far behind. He'd wanted to pop the poseur, or whatever he was, a good one in the nose. Wanted to reach over and dig into his stubbly chicken neck and throttle him. How odd. He couldn't recall ever wanting to make hash out of somebody—anybody—before. It had to be the booze.

But booze had never affected him that way before.

New Orleans approached. Maz felt it slouch toward the speeding train. The air seemed to get thicker, and to give off an ammoniac stink. The sky was ashtray gray. The egrets, dotted along the spindly cypresses of the Bonnet Carré spillway, looked like moths under a lantern-glass. But the greasy heat of the lantern's fire wasn't the sun, or its reflection in the still water. It came from the petrochem towers in the middle distance, flames like dirty blonde hair snapping in the Big One, the big storm, the one that was always coming.

In between the train and the far refineries was a waste of grasses and unmoving water, and an occasional tree (used to be more). Long-legged, broad-winged birds either stood still as tombstones or stroked themselves suddenly into the air. Maz caught some glimpses too of the actual mud that made it all possible, a bank here and there. He thought he saw also scratchings in the mud, tracks, the matchstick literature of small birds or large bugs. There was no question in Maz's mind: this was definitely where the first fish walked ashore. And there, out in the middle of it, Maz saw a house. The waste was inhabited. But what nightmares must haunt the nights of this sole inhabitant? To live out here alone, naked, in the face of whatever force would craft such a place. Too creepy for Maz. Anyplace a map was no good for seemed to him a good place to steer clear of.

Maz was closer to the map than he thought, though. One short bridge brought him back down to peopled earth. Took him over the millennia from wriggling mud to shabby suburb, and all of a sudden he could feel the pressing population, like warm and boozy breath on his neck. Yet in the visual, the ordinary prevailed. Highways, malls, cars, billboards. Not even a palm tree. Maz read the highway exit signs from his train window: Williams, Veterans, Causeway. Of course, Airport. Not much magic there. "Metairie," they called this place. A layer of Nova America wrapped tightly around the crumbly something-else of New Orleans.

The train slowed to a crawl when it hit Orleans parish, as if saying, look, you wanted to come here, look. Unlike Mississippi, New Orleans looked more beat up than he'd ever seen it. Charred frames of houses, fronts of houses with no backs. People lounging on brick steps that led to nowhere. So-called streets with holes and gashes in them, invalid cars, unable to drive, on four flat tires, windows all smashed out. Half and fully naked children cavorted in the unsound waters in the ditches lining every thoroughfare. The housing projects went on for blocks, with caved-in roofs, broken windows, too poor even for graffiti. The projects in Chicago resembled prisons. But this was worse, here they were cruelly designed to look like the Big Houses on rich plantations, or like great universities, with their smudged and chipped porches and galleries and quads. Kids bouncing around on muddy mattresses. And everywhere, puddles and sinkholes and marshy grassy lots, toothed with broken glass. The water was winning. And the garbage.

They pulled into Union Terminal only two hours behind schedule. Early. The lounge car attendant had to wake up the wild white man in the off-white togs—he'd been snoring, passed out, dribble down his chin, mouth wide open like trying to suck up whole some flailing thing in the air that nobody else could see. His young black companions had moved on. When he woke up, though, he got coherent fast. He stood up and said, "Thank you so much," dropping a few bills on the table, and brushed the sleeves of his linen suit-jacket and turned suddenly to Maz, who'd been watching him. As if he felt it, as if Maz had shot a spitball and hit him in the neck. The arrogant anachronism stared rudely, again, but this time with a look of delighted surprise. Vulgar. Like he knew Maz, like Maz was some old college (frat) buddy. Then he said, smiling big and with eyes glazing over and fluttering, almost shutting, some kind of seizure: "Well, well, I know *you're* going to have a fine time in our fair city."

Maz sidestepped him, frowning, and exited the car.

And he felt (who doesn't?) that fleeting shudder, that young lover's shy tremble, stepping into the New Orleans air for the first time all over again, after such a long absence *fly me to the moon hold my hand kiss me*. Maz felt a jump in his blood, a kick, a new thrill, stepping out to some foreign shore where the most delicious elixirs could be obtained.

Yet everything looked so shabby. Worn down and in need of paint, shoring up. Even the palmettos shading the bums on the lawn looked tired.

A red-cap directed him to a cab stand, where a car was already waiting. The driver had a white Ban-Lon zip-up polo shirt and a white mesh cap on his bald black head. He was fifty-ish and had a comfortable gut, what Maz's old Chicago pals used to call an "alderman" (and what the Mississippi black folks simply called "looking prosperous"). The cabbie greeted Maz warmly, smiled big. Took Maz's bag and sax and stowed them in the trunk, asked where he was from and how was the weather up there. When he got behind the wheel he craned his neck around and said, "Well, I know where you want to go," chuckling low, like on an inside joke, "you'll be going to the French Quarters. Am I right?"

Maz said, "Well, actually, no, I'll be staying Uptown, at the Old Orphanage Inn." He started thumbing through his wallet for an address, "On Magazine, uh, just a minute."

"That's OK, I gotcha," the driver started up the motor, "Nice place, I know that place. It's a real nice place, it is." He kept looking at Maz, in his eyes, almost, through the rear-view mirror.

"Here's the address—"

"I know where you going."

Maz settled back and enjoyed the ride *let's get lost*. It was a nice old car. Large, even for a cab. Bigger than a Caprice. Opera window. Had to be a Caddie. The brown, mildly red leather was worn and comfortably cracked. A nice easy chair. Maz chilled and let the scenery float by. Some sun had broken through the cloud banks, which had started rolling along. And his driver knew the scenic route. Took Maz down some oak-lined avenue. The branches reached over from either side of the street and touched each other. A giant drive-through arbor. They turned onto a side-street and floated through a cloud of gold pollen—spring for the live oaks (autumn for everyone else). Set back from the trees, but not by far, were the lovely houses, resting high on their elevated piers. Dressed for a ball. Frilly fascia and brackets, tall windows shuttered in purple, pink, azure, mango. A gingerbread village for hip elves. Such care for frivolity, as if naked function would be dispiriting.

The big-framed wagon rocked like a boat, dipping and rising over the uneven streets. The driver murmured gently about his daughter, who currently lived in Chicago, "... yeah, she stay up there. She a nice girl, too ..." Maz didn't hear much of the specifics, he just heard the lulling lilt of the voice *huggin' and a kissin', that's what I been missin' ... you never know how nice it seems ... when you way down south in ...*

But then he noticed a street sign. They'd just crossed Barracks. Maz never remembered Barracks being Uptown. The driver was still talking, looking at him through the rear-view mirror more than he looked at the road, then turning away when Maz caught his eye, "...You like girls, I'll gitcha girls. I know some nice ones—"

"Um, pardon me, but are we Uptown? I don't remember it being so far from the station."

The driver was quiet. The folds in the back of his neck betrayed nothing. Maz wondered if he'd heard the question.

"I wanted to go Uptown—to the Garden District, the Old Orphanage. I—"

The back of the driver's head twitched, convulsed. "'Scuse me, sir, excuse me, what are you tryin' to say?"

"Uh, just that—"

"What, you think I don't know how to drive?"

"You're driving just fine, I'm just curious about the route. Isn't this a detour?"

"A what? A detour?"

"Wait a minute." Maz paused and planned—the situation had already gotten way out of hand. And he had been so comfortable, in such a good space. Why all this sudden conflict? "I was just curious to know why we were driving through this neighborhood."

"Awww," the driver groaned, like Maz had said exactly the wrong thing. "The neighborhood." And then he spat out parodies of Maz' pronunciations, "the *naayy*-borhood! The *naayy*-borhood!"

Maz was dumbstruck. He was perched on the edge of the seat, but he just wanted to lean back again and forget the whole thing.

The sullen cabbie continued his onslaught: "Whatchu? You think I'm gonna rob you or somethin'?"

This struck Maz suddenly as a real possibility.

The driver had already slowed down. Now he glared at Maz through the rear-view. Maz back-pedaled, warily, tried to explain that of course he had no intention of offending, etcetera, but again he got cut off.

"Ain't that de bitch. White man come down here get in mah cah, think 'cause I'm a black man ah got to be some robber."

That was too much. The race card. Here Maz was trying not to hurt people's feelings when the real issue was why did he have to put up with this shit, that he obviously did nothing to provoke? He was ready to match belligerence with belligerence. He looked for the registration tag, licenses, numbers, on the dash.

And saw that there were none. Not even a radio. The car had jerked to a complete stop.

"Well you can get the hell out mah cab!" He was shouting now, and, the rear-view mirror no longer intimate enough, he'd turned around to glower at Maz directly. Maz didn't like what he saw in the man's eyes. Intimations of disproportionate revenge, bloodbath—but also a twinkle like the whole thing might be a prank.

Maz held up his hands and said, "OK, OK." The car was pulled halfway onto the sidewalk. Maz stepped out onto a brick *banquette* that sloped and shouldered like a feeding snake.

The car sped off. It was not a cab. His sax and bag were still in the trunk.

Billy Lyons said to Stagolee two men came from around the corner and walked right at him *please don't take my Stetson hat*. They took their time getting to him, but it was indubitably a beeline at nothing but himself. An older man and a younger one, a boy, really. The older one was darker, tall. He said,

"Say, man," casually, and pulled a gun out of his pants-pocket. The pants were shiny black slacks. A wide-collared paisley shirt hung over his shoulders, open and baring his chest. He had a beard, a rough goatee, the kind worn by Monk, Dolphy, Mingus. Maz thought they'd gone out of style for black men. The medium Afro was another thing Maz hadn't seen in years. The gun was small, unobtrusive. A symbol, really. Like a badge.

Billy Lyons told Stagolee but Maz knew they didn't want his life. They were businesslike. The one with the gun did the talking.

"The watch."

Maz took off his watch and gave it to the one without a gun, the kid. Maz was surprised at how easy and mellow the transaction was. So unrushed. He even took some pride in his role, in knowing the protocol.

"Billfold."

Maz handed it over. The kid stuck it in his back pocket. The man with the gun was nice enough not to aim it at Maz's head or torso. He just let it half-dangle, pointing at the ground, around Maz's feet. Maz felt oddly comfortable. He thought he'd try to communicate with them. No sermonizing, though. He just said, "Y'know, there's money in that wallet, but, the rest of it, y'all don't need it. I mean, credit cards, I'm just gonna cancel 'em, you won't be able to use them—"

The kid hissed. "Not if they don't find yo' body, bitch."

But the older one made a mild gesture and the kid

moaned a "maannn" and handed the wallet over to Dolphy goatee. The mentor stuck his gun back in his pants and went through the wallet, yanked the bills (about twenty bucks), eyed a few cards, and handed it back to Maz. "OK, Pete," he said. "Got anything else?" When Maz shook his head and shrugged his shoulders, he said, "Check 'im out" and the apprentice patted Maz down lightly.

The kid wore a blue tank-top with a yellow number—15—and tight, fancy stitched faded jeans. His shoulders were downy soft, velvety, like the backside of a magnolia leaf, same color, too, a red-tinted brown, like a soft old worn wet brick. He glanced up at Maz and for the briefest flicker the eyes weren't hostile. They were just eyes meant to meet, take in, process, accept. Long lashes, boyish cheek. Full lips that faded to a tender pink smack in the exact middle of his kisser.

Maz wanted to kiss him. Yes kiss him *a huggin' and a kissin' that's what I been missin'* He wanted it so bad he almost did it. But then the eyes went that shackle color again and the kid said, "Whatchu lookin' at, fag? Let's shoot his ass!"

He couldn't have been more than thirteen. Now an insolent punk again. Maz wanted the boy back. He knew it was in there somewhere. The punk brought his twisted face right up an inch from Maz's and glared right in his eyes—he had to stand on his toes to do it. Maz knew not to return the gaze. He kept his lids low.

But the one in control, the one with the gun, made the kid step off and addressed Maz like a teacher giving a homework assignment, friendly but firm: "Go that way, now. Don't turn around. We watching."

So Maz walked in the direction he was told. As instructed, he didn't look back, just kept his eyes on the brick patchwork rolling out bumpy smooth under his feet.

He stepped casually, a stroll, but thought hard. Mind ramped up, full capacity. He often asked himself about the old saw he heard growing up about God always having a purpose in mind for people and what happened to them. He wondered about the purpose of the experience. Did it have one? To teach him a lesson or make him feel a certain way? How did he feel?

He felt OK. He felt good. He had his life. He was in New Orleans. What about losing his stuff? So? So he had no possessions to fetter him. He had his credit cards. And the air was being mighty nice to him. It was the right temperature and moisture to feel like, and with that fragrance—sweet olive?—to feel like the rub of soft but committed hands, in a blossom-strewn bath. The weedy brick sidewalk was a low gliding Turkish rug. He began humming "Night in Tunisia." Then he started singing it. A group of beer-drinkers on and around a door stoop shouted encouragement at him— "Da's right, get down! ... Check 'im out!" Laughing up a strange black stew of appreciation and ridicule. Then the words to the song didn't cut it anymore. His mouth started scatting all over the place, up and down charged bop intervals, the augmented fourth, the flat 6. He was on a cruise, a river cruise, a pleasure cruise on a star. He'd hit a groove. Tripping down Rampart Street singing a song *the same moon above you aglow with a cool evening light, that shining at night in ...*

II. FOOLS RUSH IN 🎺 MEDIUM SLOW, SWINGING ♪

Fools rush in
Where angels fear to tread
And so I come to you, my love
My heart above my head
 —as sung by Johnny Hartman, Feb. 18, 1956, at Chicago's *Basin Street*, after hours

Almost nightfall. Almost. In between the cracks—the best place. When day can't throw in the towel but night hasn't quite stepped up either, not come, gone, and disappointed. The best part of the night is before it falls, when it's still the endless galaxy every night—properly watered—*could* be. In theory. Maybe tonight would be a big one, with everything. Everything could happen all over again. And Maz had thought until today that all he had left were small, isolated crumbs of somethings.

He'd lost his taste for Garden District fare like the Old Orphanage. Downtown seemed like the place to *be*. He crossed Rampart, wandered into the Quarter and looked around. There was bound to be some little guest-house. What an unlikely name "Barracks" was for the charming, shady domestic lane he walked in. The tinkles and hollow clunks of wind chimes, metal, glass, and bamboo, sidled up into his ear in a most magnanimous fashion. Another track was laid down, like scurrying tiny feet, by the fallen oak leaves pushed along by the wind. Down in the bass an occasional throaty ship's horn reverberated the sidewalk and his feet. Also coming from the river was the circus gaiety of a calliope, jamming "You Are My Sunshine." A silly ditty of a song, but a governor wrote it, and what other state besides Louisiana would produce a song-writing governor?

The architecture had the vintage postcard look: earth-toned Creole Cottages and brightly painted Double Shotguns fast along the narrow sidewalk. More elaborate homes stood back behind high walls. Maz paused in front of one and gazed through the peephole of the gate. The peephole itself was a thing of high craftsmanship, a face-sized arabesque of frilly iron, painted an ethereal powder blue. The marble stoop at his feet bore a depression worn by centuries of footfalls. Rainwater had pooled in this micro-pond and, already, green moss had formed and tiny bugs flecked the surface. Nobody had stepped here lately. The courtyard within, however, was well-tended, a gardener's triumph. It was shaded by a massive magnolia, and by the high brick walls of adjoining three-story townhomes. Downright dark, actually, and Maz marveled that the sun, even at its long Gulf zenith, managed to angle in enough rays for the obvious photosynthesis that took place here. Great urns supported a range of plant life: lemon trees, ornamental pears, white and purple hibiscus, miniature azaleas. A giant rusty cistern in the middle was overgrown with some kind of lotus. Thin blades of swamp iris fanned across the border between patio and house.

The house itself, though, was in need of attention. The wide gallery listed dangerously on one side, the whole thing needed paint, and the roofing slates were chipped and slipping. Maz saw what appeared to be some kind of hill behind the house, but this seemed unlikely given the topography. No, it wasn't a hill. It was another building. It only looked like a hill because the roof was verdant as a cow pasture. It even supported a few yellow flowers in addition to the ropes of leaves. Too bad he couldn't check in here. He wondered what the structure must be like on the inside. Like living in the earth. Probably nothing remained under the verdure besides a few supports and crossbeams, maybe a few stubborn shingles.

He was suddenly distracted by movement in the front building—the "Big House," since the overgrown thing behind had obviously been a slave quarter. The place was inhabited, after all. By cats, anyway. Which meant someone had to feed them. He counted two, five, seven? They were everywhere, they owned the gallery. They all looked kin, too. All black, or mostly black with white socks and undersides.

One of them strode resolutely along the rickety wooden banister, mouthing a twitching lizard.

Considering that humans—with the obvious exception of a professional gardener—didn't seem to come here, Maz considered jumping the gate and joining the cats, but a tap came on his shoulder and he jerked around. There on the sidewalk was a short black man in t-shirt and jeans holding

37

his hands up in a placating gesture.

"Hol' on, now, hol' on," he stammered. "My name is Willard Johnson. Now I live at thirteen-eighteen Arts Street, and you could check the address, I swear."

Maz nodded, wondered what the little man wanted.

"My sister is in the hospital and my car just got towed. Now, don't be scared now."

"I'm not scared." He wasn't. The man seemed too nervous to mug him. Or was that, too, subterfuge?

"Now anyone will tell you, I am an honest man. I am an honest man."

He seemed to be waiting for Maz to jump into the conversation, so Maz said, "OK."

"I just need five dollars and eighty cents, sir, so I can get my kids over by my mama's house. I'm just trying to take care of my kids."

"Oh," Maz said, his part suddenly dawning on him, "Oh, sure." He dug in his pocket.

"God bless you, sir, God bless you."

But he had no money, because he had just been robbed. Yes. He shook his head, held up his hands, shrugged. "I'm sorry."

The man cocked his head and eyed Maz. He looked on the verge of tears. Was it real?

"Sorry," Maz said again, this time more forcefully. "I just got mugged, if you wanna know the truth."

But the man stood his ground. Just stood there looking at Maz, not saying a word. His expression was like a guy who'd just been insulted but was too well-bred to make a big deal out of it.

Maz mumbled another "sorry" and, though he wanted to spend more time with the cats, felt it best to move on down the street, since the beggar had apparently laid claim to that particular spot of sidewalk. A few yards later he shot a glance back and saw that he still stood there, still looked sullenly after him.

Maz rounded the corner of Dauphine and saw a simple double shotgun painted bright yellow with alternating navy and light-blue trim. Hanging above the door was a sign: *Dauphine Courtyard Inn.* He rang the bell and was admitted by a neatly dressed inconspicuous gay man his own age. Yes, they had a room. Did they take cards? Of course.

He checked in. He didn't have any bags. His host remarked that this wasn't unusual at all, that when New Orleans calls, one must go, bags or not. He led Maz upstairs, and Maz said he hadn't realized from the street that this "shotgun" had a second story. "Yes," said Wendell, his host, "it's actually what we call a 'camelback.'" He said it was built in the 1920s, but all the furniture was antiques. Maz's room was sterile and fake-homey as a Bed and Breakfast in Wisconsin (antiques or no), except for a framed Mardi Gras poster depicting the devil or a satyr fucking an amplebodied woman on a couch.

No television. Good.

He thought about taking a shower but he'd just have to put his old dirty clothes on again so he decided against it. He did discover, though, after he'd started to take off his pants, that he had thirty bucks in his left back pocket. The boy mugger's pat-down hadn't been sensitive enough. Thirty bucks in the bank was nothing. But on your person it meant something. What would he buy with it?

The room was on the small side. Its most prominent feature was a wide casement window opposite the bed. The whole chamber, in fact, seemed framed around the window. Like a loge, it invited the inhabitant to consider what lay outside as a spectacle. Maz unlatched the window and pushed it open, leaned his head out and heard a gurgling fountain on the patio. The water trickled from the uplifted hand and down the body of a nude bronze youth with eyes trained on Maz' window. A few cast-iron chairs and tables, all empty, surrounded the fountain.

What was the water saying? Get on out there and party.

Sounded good to Maz. He had energy, lots of energy, even if he had no idea where it came from. He laughed at his recent predilection for napping afternoons. He couldn't fathom why anyone would ever want to do anything like nap. Restlessness is good, all it is, is energy. Anxiety would be a misinterpretation.

So he hit the streets again. Miraculously, the sun had still not given up the ghost. The shadows cast long, the streets were dusky, but the sky still gave off light. Couldn't part with its own brilliance. A sun that didn't know when to quit, refused to go to bed when told. "Fuck him," Maz grunted—though he sympathized.

He remembered only scattered place-names from his previous visits, but one corner that stuck in his head was Bourbon and Dumaine—used to be you could get reefer (or whatever) there. He wanted to get high. It had been ... years. He didn't remember where exactly the corner was but it appeared suddenly, which reminded him: the Quarter had always been that way, scrunched against itself, close, breathy, but snaky, weaselly, too. You were always right next to everything but could wander all day looking for a specific point and never find it.

Yet here it was. The weed corner. And it looked like the same guy from years ago, too. A long, mild, sleepy-lidded face. Different clothes, but the same age *three time seven, just turn twenty-one, got a big fat woman* The dealer walked Maz a few yards down Dumaine and Maz said, "Y'know I was smoking this stuff probably before your dad was born."

"Ain't no point in quittin' now, huh?"

"Well, I did quit."

The kid didn't say anything to that, just kept glancing up and down the street and holding out a hand with three little dime bags for Maz to choose from. Maz selected one and paid up the twenty dollars—he couldn't figure out why they still called them dimes. He said, "Y'know, my first record, and I'm talking the nineteen-forties, was called 'reefer-man'. It was a big thing then."

"Well, well, you a old-timer," he laughed (it seemed genuine) and headed back toward the corner, "be cool."

Oh, I'm cool, Maz thought. Yep. But it's time to turn the heat up. He stepped into the first bar he came to—he had to walk two feet—to get a cold one to go.

It was a gay place. He liked the bartender, the way he said, "Whatchu want, honey?" He enjoyed watching him draw the beer, swivel-hipped with his dated feathered dishwater hair—something sexy about trailer trash. Not the right target, though, this one. He didn't want to fuck the guy, he just dug watching and knowing that, after all, there was nothing to keep him from fucking whom-the-fuck he pleased. Was there? No reason not to. The possibility opened up like one of Ella's gliding hummed runs, a whisper first, then stretching through throat and then nasal, then head voice, ending up open wide on a forceful big-mouthed vowel *ain't never loved but three men, my ... my ... and the man who wrecked my life*

New Orleans is for lovers. He'd sit on the possibility for a while. He liked just having it there, like a six-pack in the fridge. So he got his cup and smiled at the bartender and they smiled at each other and it was a good feeling. But he couldn't stay. He had a date with the night air.

He headed out and picked up some double wide rolling papers and rolled the whole dime-bag into one and sat on a bench on the levee—the "Moonwalk," they called it—and smoked the fucker. Watched possibilities floating up from the Big River like bubbles in champagne *goin' down to the river, gonna take my rockin' chair*. What had whispered from the fountain at his guest-house was now a whole big body of (brown) water lapping at his feet, in the bass. In Chicago it had been frozen ice.

He wanted to get in there. He wanted to feel the force of the river, but still be in control.

But tonight he just wanted to catch some jazz. He'd picked up a *Gambit*—more colorful but a lot thinner than Chicago's *Reader*—so he flipped to the music section and found the name he was looking for: Berta Bredeaux. One of the champagne bubbles attained the air and became a plan. If he hadn't been in such a weird state before he left Chicago, he would have called and told Berta in advance. He could have crashed on her couch. Or at least she would have offered. But now he was here, he figured he'd swing by and crash her show—at the *Kozy Kove*, on Frenchmen Street, a nice strolling distance away.

But there was time yet before she started up, so Maz decided to check Jackson Square and see what was doing in front of the Cathedral. He crossed Decatur Street and saw that it looked more developed since his last visit. The 1980s had finally arrived. It had been a place of dive bars, winos, and the lowest sort of hookers. That era was, however, clearly past. It was nice to see a viable economy afoot, but he didn't like the style. He had no idea how any economy could support the number of tacky souvenir storefronts that crowded every block. T-shirt shops and bars alike spewed loud, too forcibly upbeat forgeries of the local music. Into a street that would have been much more aesthetically satisfying had every door been padlocked.

Every place was too brightly lit, full of anxious people trying desperately to ladle as much expensive, pre-fabricated "fun" into their mouths and shopping bags as they could on their short allotted "vacation" time. The worst were the drinking establishments—Maz refused to honor them with the term "bar." Here the neon, the paint, and even the drinks themselves screeched in a cacophony of purple, pink, sea-foam and a multitude of other grotesque shades. The appropriate expression to don while consuming these wares was, Maz knew (and saw), a maniacal grin poised on the brink of violence. Not "bars," but they definitely moved the booze. Daiquiris, namely, in an array of colors to rival nail polish, served from a bank of dispensers like Icees at a 7-11. You could get a beer if you were willing to suck it out of a magenta, fuchsia, or lime yard of plastic. Maz spotted a d.j. on a platform at the back of one of these places—the doors were all wide open—but he wasn't spinning records. Instead he pumped up the crowd with admonitions like, "Is everyone ready to PARTY? It's PARTY TIME!"

Maz was relieved to get back to the Square. The shops in the Pontalba buildings, now closed, were kept in check by zoning, apparently. A few artists lingered next to their easels, charcoals, caricatures. A few tarot readers, too, but the main attraction was down by the Cabildo, where Maz saw a crowd assembled. He hoped it was music, rather than acrobats or magic or whatever. Yeah, a trad jazz outfit.

They sounded OK. They were young, probably school kids. They were doing "St. James Infirmary." One sousaphone, a bass trombone, an older white guy on clarinet (probably sitting in). Bass drum and snare. Maz wondered where the requisite trumpet was hiding. They had a ragged trad sound, but the sousaphone player seemed bored. Maz took more interest in the scene than the music. The arcade of the Cabildo stood directly behind and framed them nicely, back-lit them with flickering gaslight. In front of them was a white plastic bucket for tips. To the left was a Lucky Dog vendor, looking as drunk or disoriented by medication as they always had. To the right, a row of white girls in school uniforms—plaid skirts, white blouses, an occasional maroon sweater, saddle shoes—filed into the cathedral. They seemed oblivious to the band, audience, air. A thin white-haired nun followed behind them, but she looked around more. She actually caught Maz's eye and said good evening, with that New Orleanian smile that seemed so real. But how could it be? How could they smile at strangers so much all the day long and still mean it?

The band's audience numbered about twenty, and they all looked very much alike. They were the same people from the daiquiri places. Shorts, souvenir T (usually tucked in), athletic shoes or the most hi-tech kind of flip-flop. And yes, video-cameras. One grouping, though, seemed to be Europeans. The men wore long pants with dress shoes and sports shirts; the women blouses tucked into skirts. Maz overheard their talk—German. Then there was a cluster of young Japanese hipsters who wore tight-fitting t-shirts and jeans, in tasteful colors, though the hair of one of them was dyed a bright red. Up against the gate of the Square, and not to be confused with the music enthusiasts, lounged three gutter punks, in their black tatters, sharing a six-pack of *Milwaukee's Best*. They had a ragged dog with them, too, for whom they all tilted their beer cans from time to time.

Turning back toward the band, Maz saw a player he had missed. He sat a bit apart, aloof, it seemed, on his instrument case. The instrument was, in fact, the missing trumpet. A cornet, actually. He was a bit younger than the others. He was also better dressed and, Maz noted with an inner quaver, much more attractive. His skin tone perched at the soft cusp between red and brown, neither light-skinned nor dark, but a solid middle. His hair was cropped close, which allowed the perfectly sculpted head to arise from the torso with a plain, unadorned dignity. He had long lashes, light brown, mutable eyes, and a noble nose of even lines, whose tip bent ever so slightly towards the exact middle of his mouth. The lips seemed maybe better suited for trombone than trumpet. They were full, and became slightly pinker at the center, as if a clever darting tongue had inexorably lightened the pigment there. When he stood, he did it all in one smooth motion, not a faltering arm and leg at a time. His shirt was yellow with black dots. That and his build—a runner's body—put Maz in mind of a cheetah. The shirt was silk, so it draped easily, hung straight down over broad chest and tight stomach, and then, in back, rested on the gentle but marked curve of his high round ass, couched seamlessly in brown pleated slacks.

After a brief sidelong glance, to see if others had noticed this phenomenon of American nature—they apparently hadn't—Maz found that he couldn't turn away. The cornet hung limp from his left hand, while the fingers of his right played lightly over keys, spit-valve. The fingers were long but not bony. Nothing on him was bony: a wholesome layer of effortless muscle hugged his entire frame. He appeared to not even be listening to his fellows. He appeared to be wandering—but not lost—in a music of his own unselfconscious imagination.

But when the band kicked into "Little Liza Jane," the young musician put horn to lips, breathed in some soundless air, and strolled to a spot out in front, the band a few feet behind, and blew. The sounds were as effortless as his gait. The boy had grace. The four-note melody came out like everyday conversation. Something like, "Did you catch the game last night?" The ineffable hook was in the timbre. The right admixture of gruff breathiness and full, though dark, rounded tone. His attacks were soft, as if barely tongued at all, or with the middle of his tongue against the palette only. He darted up a scale to a higher register for his solo, which came hard on the heels of the chorus. The scale was almost sloppy, lazy, yet clear. Fluid. Like those wordless expressions he'd heard New Orleans people use with such precision, the "mmmm's" and the "aahh's." He attacked a bit more sharply for the one-note rhythmic figure that formed the heart and climax of his solo, but still gave the impression of holding back. Just sparring. Like a well-fed

47

cheetah at rest, no need to burn up the grass for dinner, or for the cameras. He lowered his horn and nodded at the applause of the audience. A German dropped a fin in the bucket and got an extended nod for his generosity. Maz was glad he had no cash—he wasn't sure if he could handle eye-contact with this particular cat, not right now.

The clarinetist was taking a solo when another sound intruded. Maz wasn't sure it was intended to be music at first but it came back in regular, though ugly, intervals, so he guessed it was. A tourist had taken up one of those long plastic party-trumpets and actually had the chutzpah to join in with the real musicians. As a matter of fact, he soon occupied the spot just vacated by the singular cornetist. The guy stood there, in a white baseball cap and ropes of Mardi Gras beads around his neck (in October), and blew into his long plastic contraption. Bleated. Maz was peeved that the band didn't tell him to step off. Quite the contrary—they shouted encouragement at him. The gorgeous cornet player fell in right next to him, horn tucked under his arm, and began clapping out the beat. The tourist was ecstatic. He jerked up his knees awkwardly and tried to swivel his hips at the same time. He stumbled but kept bellowing through the plastic thing, more and more frantically and with even less attention to the rhythm set by the others.

The band just let him play himself out and collapse on a bench. At which point he received wild applause from his countrymen—the Americans—and from the band, too. The white clarinetist congratulated him on his enthusiasm.

Hearing the reed player's English accent, Maz realized, with great annoyance, that the white Americans were the only people here that he had a real dislike for. They were babies. Fat, thoughtless babies with a boundless sense of entitlement, made sadistic by their signature art form, television.

Maz quit the Square in a huff. He couldn't bear to see these American babies so pandered to. Especially not by this cheetah who seemed to have sprung, fully formed, from Maz's own private fantasy world.

The *Kozy Kove* hadn't changed much since Maz had last played it. It had been glitzier then. Ten, twenty years ago? Couldn't remember. Now it was a little shabby. Well-worn. That was good. It was now a jazz "institution"—even in New Orleans, apparently, jazz institutions sprang up as fast as they disappeared. Berta's picture was by the door, in a little frame, lit from above, the word "tonite" handwritten below. In the picture her eyes were closed, her face angled downward in a semi-profile, lots of shadow. Black-and-white, of course. Nostalgic, like the *Kove* itself, with its tiny round tables with little shaded lamps. A museum or library quiet suffused the place. People spoke in hushed tones. Being a bar—a real bar—the sound of clinking glassware and ice added to the decor. Beyond the narrow, low-ceilinged barroom, a Chinese screen, carved and lacquered, set apart a larger room, with stage and about thirty little tables. The waiters—all attractive young men—stood along the walls in

49

French aprons.

But Berta's piano is what transformed the plain room into a place swelling with meaning. Her big rich block chords, like Red Garland's (a ballad, big hands), were the furthest thing from shabby. A plush rug, silk pillows, a wash of coppery light. Berta was a sophisticate. A Sophisticated Lady. Maz wondered if anybody had ever called her "esoteric," like they'd maligned him. He thought not and he thought he knew why. Of course, it was always the same reason.

Maz took a seat right up front, but she didn't notice him. Didn't interact much with her audience. Not a showman-type performer. A cool spirit. She hardly ever looked up over the piano, and when she did it was at the other members of her trio: a drummer and bass man Maz didn't recognize. Young cats. Apprentices. One of them white—the drummer.

Berta finished up the set with some old barrel-house boogie-woogie thing. Very New Orleans. Professor Longhair, Booker, Eddie Bo, Dr. John. Her bass player stopped in the middle of it and just stood there grinning nervously—she'd departed from the expected changes and gone off on some convoluted sub fantasy. It got Maz hyped. His knee was jerking up and down and he knew he looked like the caricature of a jazz druggie (speed-freak) in some forties movie. He was grinning and nodding like that, too. "Yeah. Yeah." If only he'd worn a beret.

Applause (from the ten-person crowd). She got up and stepped off the stage, smiled and wagged a finger at the bassist, chatted with the folks at the nearest table. She wore a reddish earth-colored linen pants ensemble, loose and diaphanous. It set off the clay tones in her skin well. A wealth of thick stone beads draped from her neck. She continued toward the bar and Maz crept up behind her and announced, "The versatility of Dame Berta!"—he knew no-one had called her that lately, not since the '50s, when she had been a minor R&B diva.

She didn't turn or slow down, but she must have heard him. She made it to the bar. She said to the bartender, her face tilted slightly backward, "Now, C. W., I know the man behind me is at least as old as me and maybe older—could you tell me is he fine? 'Cause I ain't got time for no not-fine."

The bartender smiled—Maz knew Berta was smiling, too—and said, "... mmmm, fine? Well, he's tall."

Maz: "Hey!"

Then the bartender seemed to recognize him, "Oh ..."

But Berta spun around and said it, "Maz Mazooki!" It's what she'd always called him since ...? He couldn't remember.

She gave him a big, deep hug, accompanied by a long and variegated "mmmmmm." Then she said, "Now, sit!" and they took seats at the bar. She told him how wonderful he looked, young. He said he liked her dreds (a new thing).

"Well, you gots to do something when you hit fifty. Change something. The alternative is atrophy, Mister—or is it Reverend?—" (she laughed airily)—"kooky Mazooki."

She slurped through her straw. The sight of her face filled Maz with warmth—he had apparently missed her. Yes, he had. If his feelings were more assertive in the hierarchy of his personality, he'd have just felt one day that he missed her—but that part of himself was so often AWOL. He needed to fix that somehow.

Berta had a round, pleasant face, that could be drawn as a collection of different sized circles. Prominent cheekbones, nose, mouth, chin, all rounded. She managed to stay so youthful, too. Part of it was the urchinish gap between her two front teeth, and the freckles.

"Atrophy…" Maz mused. "Well that's not what you're doing. You were flying up there."

She asked him how long he'd been in town and where he was staying, but he couldn't remember the name of his guest house. She sniffed at his face. "I can get you better grass than that, Maz."

"Still smokin' huh?"

She lowered the corners of her mouth for drama. "I'm gettin' around a little bit still. Not like you though. You fly down to New Orleans, you don't tell me, you crash my venue, you're all … *high*. You makin' me feel old, Maz!"

"Well, now that you say it, I do feel younger now than I did yesterday."

"Wait till tomorrow morning, then you'll feel older than you did the day before."

"That's the idea." He lifted his glass to her. "I'm a bubble in champagne."

"You a bubble alright." More slurping with her straw, without lifting the glass from the bar. It was some kind of gesture, supposed to mean something.

"You *do* look younger, though. Got your horn?"

Maz said, "You look younger, too." Actually, it seemed more like she just hadn't aged. "Or maybe you just don't look any older."

She laughed at this, and said, "Well, y'know black don't crack."

He couldn't figure out what she meant so he didn't say anything. She squinted at him and threw out a facial expression that normally goes with a shrug. She asked after his horn again, and his horn began to seem to him like a bothersome wife. He chuckled and said, "Well..." and looked down at a cigarette butt on the floor. Cigarettes. He needed a pack. He waved the bartender over.

Berta just kept beaming a question mark at him with her eyes.

"No, you know, I'm laying off the sax for a while."

"Doin' what?" She scrunched up her face in disbelief, gawked at him, "What, you a singer now?"

"Yeah, actually, that's what I've been doing. Really."

The bartender put a pack of Pall Malls in front of him, what he used to smoke back in the Division Street days.

"A crooner? Git outta here! Really?"

He lit up and nodded, eyebrows high with a surging confidence, possibility. Good Pall Mall tobacco smoke hovered in and around him, telling him "Yes, you can do it,

53

yes."

"And here I thought a change in hair was gonna be enough," Berta said. "I'm gonna have to quit keyboardin' and take up banjo or something. I mean I already did the singing, remember?"

"Yeah, and you stopped and here I am picking it up."

"Mmmp," she assented, "I *would* sing still, and I do, y'know, by my lonesome. But I'm worried my voice isn't too strong anymore."

"Well, that doesn't matter, right? As long as it has character?"

"What kind of character is what matters."

She asked him if he wanted to sit in and he said sure. She patted him on the shoulder and drifted off to use the bathroom or socialize or stand off alone somewhere. She was in that gig mindset of never stay on one thing too long.

He looked at his pack of Pall Malls and remembered that he hadn't asked for this brand—even though he was glad to get them. He hadn't paid for them, or his drink either. Well, he probably got set up because he was with Berta—maybe because the bartender knew him. But then he looked up from the bar and saw, down at the other end, a man staring at him with a shit-eating grin. The man giggled and winked and raised his glass. He looked like some college buddy (frat-type) congratulating him for appearing to hit on Berta. The man was well beyond college age, though, with his shock of silver hair. Wore a loose fitting suit, which seemed to be white at first but then looked more like a pale lavender.

Maz thought of old Jack Teagarden again. He'd actually been rude to him. Some benefit gala concert with the Earl Hines All-Stars. Jack T. would actually pass out in his chair right up on stage. Something had happened to him. Maz remembered standing up to take a solo (K.C.? The Biltmore?) when Teagarden slumped half out of his chair and almost knocked him over. Maz had to stand up nice and straight and not move around much during his solo, so that Jack. T. would be balanced just right and not hit the floor clattering with his 'bone and his lanky self. During that same performance, though, Jack T. sang *A Hundred Years From Today* and Maz felt a certain kind of fear for the first time, a vague psychic cramp that sparked him to get hip, political, involved, to shake a fist whenever he wasn't shaking his horn, as if being tied into the life-line of some mass happening could prevent it: the fear of being the age he was now. And all the while, some unfinished business inside, like a forgotten debt piling up interest.

And now, at the *Kozy Kove* a social eon later, he realized for the first time why he'd said to Teagarden's face, his voice cracking with the adrenalin of the doubtful, "Get a grip on yourself and get a bath." Teagarden didn't respond. Except with a look, a look that Maz knew he'd given so much that he was bored with having to keep giving it. At Monterrey a few years later Jack's brother Charlie just said, "Well, he must've been having a bad day. Jack has bad days sometimes." Anyway, by then, at Monterey, Big T. looked much better and Maz wanted to join with Gerry Mulligan in a symbolic sitting-in with him—but couldn't get up the nerve. Teagarden died soon after.

Who was he to go off on Big T? A true great, and a white player who earned the respect of black players. And who was he to judge another man's medicine? Maz suddenly feared it was his turn, his turn for a young hipper-than-thou white cat to put him in his place. And the weepy sick frail feeling came on again.

So he tried to avoid the bartender's eye. As well as the eye of the man in the lavender suit—they were both waiting for Maz to notice them. The bartender hovered nearby, seemed about to approach him. He looked like a guy who wanted to be somebody. Probably a young musician still in the struggling, starving stages—where he might stay his whole life. If he asked Maz, Maz would tell him: "Take some advice from an old pro. Don't play jazz. Don't even go there."

The man in the suit, though, Maz did know him—well, recognized him. From the lounge on the train. There sat the tell-tale panama hat on the bar next to him. He seemed to have freshened up considerably, though, and in such a short span of time. Maz decided to ignore him again and turned away from the bar. He went back to his spot next to the stage. Berta was starting up again. But Maz' mind wandered back to the bar. Maybe the bartender was a fan, trying to find a way to show the love. Or not? Maz tried not to care. Fuck praise, it's no different than ridicule. Fans, enemies, stalkers.

Why had he gotten so bitter all of a sudden? He worked through it with the help of Berta's bitchy rendition of *Straight, No Chaser*.

Then she played *Don't Call It Love*.

A drink later he felt better. Berta called him to the stage. "We have a special surprise for y'all tonight, at no extra charge—that's because it's a surprise for me, too." Stage grin, stage chuckle. "Ladies and Gentlemen, saxophone great Maz Mazooki ... making his *vocal* debut." Surprised looks, mild, non-committal applause. But did they really know him?

Maz called *Sleepin' Bee*. They had to stop and start again when he realized he'd given his alto key—the wrong one for his voice. *When a bee lies sleeping/ In the palm of your hand ...*

But after Berta wrapped it up with a bass growl and a little sopranino trill up top, she clearly quoted her bass-line from *Don't Call It Love* and snickered—her bass player caught it and snickered, too. What? The drummer didn't seem to get it. Maz didn't get it either, but for some reason he didn't like it. It made somebody out in the audience crack up, too: a tall lanky shape in a broad-brim hat. The man from Amtrak. Standing, swaying in the shadows at the rear.

Maz ignored him a third time.

But when they did *Just One of Those Things*, Maz felt the waking up thing again, the rudder in the river, cutting through, working it. Alive. The groove. *If we thought a bit of the end of it, when we started painting the town too hot not to cool down* He forgot he was singing. He pulled it off. Dreamt the dream and woke up to real applause.

Berta praised him. Said his voice had character. Said he'd hit on a good new thing. Something he could grow some more with. He was a new thing again, and jazz was about staying a new thing. Generation, re-generation. An evolving species in time-lapse. Staying on top was about being constantly a step ahead of your own heart-beat.

He took his seat and basked in the glow and Berta winked at him and played (of course) *In The Afterglow*. Like the sky in New Orleans, like the sun that refused to shut its eyes, no matter how late.

She finished up the set, though, with something that disturbed him. It didn't seem right or appropriate—Baroque counterpoint, some Bach theme. She mish-mashed Baroque and jazz harmonic concepts so that both were disfigured, ultimately unrecognizable. Both traditions ended up lessened, impoverished, degraded, by the mix. Maz thought she'd finally gone too far.

He tried to talk to her about it after she wrapped up. "You were all over the place," he critiqued, "You think you can do that, I mean, really? I mean, you just keep going off in all directions, don't you?"

"Well, I just keep branching out, yes, and ... one has to. Don't *you*? Isn't that exactly what you've always done? Including tonight?"

"I've always done new things. Branching out? I wouldn't call it branching out. Because where are you then? Where's your center?"

"Mr. Barrel of Surprises. I've got a surprise for you and I hope you can handle it: the branches *are* your center, Maz."

Maz tried to grasp what she meant, he looked up from the bar to shake his eyes up in hopes that it would spark something—but there was nothing. He just didn't get it. And then he saw him, the man from the train (stalker?), tipping his hat. He had sidled up right next to them at the bar. Had been listening, without announcing himself. Snake.

"Well, Maz—or should I say *Reverend?*—Mazewski, I do believe you **do** have a bee in your hand!" The gaunt fop extended his palm.

Maz looked at it and said, "If I could find out who started that reverend shit I'd shoot his ass."

Berta looked shocked, though not without the air of amusement that never left her.

The man smiled, like he'd done it on the train: his eyes rolled up into his lids and buzzed there. He said, through silent laughter, "Sometimes appellations apply in spite of their origins."

Berta said, "Mister Leggit! The places you show up!"

"Why dontcha call me Davis, Berta?"

"I thought you liked being called mister." Her grin was one Maz had seen before, a lot, but he couldn't place it. It was a wise fool smirk, a mask. For white people. Could he trust her? Or was she like the others?

"Who you been talking to, girl?" laughed the man,

Leggit.

Berta laughed, too, a throaty sarcastic laugh.

Maz finally shook hands and introduced himself and met Davis Leggit, who offered him a card. Maz tucked it into his back pocket, where he planned to leave it until it was the laundry lady's problem.

Leggit said, "I believe it would be appropriate for me to express the honor ..." He trailed off and looked bored with himself, "uh, and privilege, eh fuck."

"What?"

Then he waved his hand in a way that said 'fuck it' better than his words could, and added, "Like to buy you one," gesturing at the other end of the bar, as if hinting at some illicit deal. "A lot I'd like to talk to you about." Then he sauntered off. The best saunter Maz had ever seen.

Berta told him Davis Leggit was a DJ on WARM, did a show featuring the new marching band sounds. "Knows a lot of the young pups, some kind of connection," Berta said, *"Wild Bunch, Funky Invaders, Soul Assassins."*

Maz didn't know about the new marching band sounds. Berta hammed up a shocked expression. Then she said, "Isn't it funny how stuff keeps happening even if nobody's looking?"

But not for me Berta had to go. Maz asked her why and she said because she was getting old. He didn't care, though. He was glad to get her off his back. She wasn't the reason he came down here. She asked him how long he'd be around. He said, "Indefinitely." A phone call was promised and she was gone.

Can't you hear the pitter-pat and Maz pulled up a stool next to Davis Leggit. For once he didn't fight the magnet. But his interest in Leggit wasn't sexual. Well, it was, somehow, just not focused on him directly.

The new marching band sounds. What were they?

"Maaazzz," Leggit breathed, "I'm so pleased to have the pleasure. Drinkin'?"

"Uh, yes." Maz swept his eyes around the *Kozy Kove*, as if he'd just arrived.

"I know you *are*, my question concerns what is your preference?"

Maz couldn't remember what he'd been drinking, couldn't remember what he liked, even. "I don't know. What's good?"

Leggit guffawed suddenly and loudly and slapped Maz on the back. "There's a lot that's good. You see, that's why folks have so much trouble deciding in life which good thing it is, exactly, that they want."

"What are you having?"

Leggit didn't answer, he just raised his eyebrows and nodded and twirled a finger at the bartender, who seemed to have been watching them for a while now.

Leggit was a talker. Practiced and animated. Knew a lot about jazz. Knew a fair bit about Maz, too. But when he listened, he *seemed* to really listen. His eyes tapping always right on the door, with intricate head movements that seemed to fine-tune his attentiveness. He reminded Maz of

61

that close-up photograph of LBJ giving some senator the "Johnson treatment." Like he wanted to make a deal. *Hey, hey, LBJ* the words Maz had built into an ostinato refrain on stage, to 12-bar blues, when he still played sax, when he still could, at Grant Park, Chicago, August 28, 1968, in the sun, sleepless. In a sudden but deep flash, like an undertow, the face in front of him was Johnson's, not Leggit's, and Maz felt faint, exhausted. But it went away as Leggit's banter lapped on. Such a pleasing voice, like gurgling water. Soft on the ear, even when he took it upon himself to point out Maz's shortcomings.

"Your problem, venerable *maestro*, is that you find yourself always uncomfortable in the present."

What was he talking about? And why did he seem to know Maz so well?

"This is because you have been misled by the chimera of ... what is the term? *Social responsibility*, I believe."

Maz's hackles went up. "Responsibility is a chimera?"

"For some, yes. Not for the wretches of the earth, of course, for whom it's a matter of self-interest. And not for our elected wretches, who sacrifice their very cocks on the altar of mediocrity."

"You're not being very clear-"

"Clarity is for schoolteachers," he barked.

"Okayyy ..." Maz wasn't sure that an appeal to reason would work on this effete reptile, but he took a swing anyway, kept it simple: "What's wrong with leaving the world slightly better off than when you came?"

"Go for it, Christian soldier. But remember what Caesar said to Antony: Beware yon Cassius. He sees no theater, Maz, he drinks no wine. He gets no boody."

"I don't remember that last part."

"Ah, but that's the most important part, my Chicago *paisano*. Best damn line Shakespeare ever wrote, too." Leggit had to drink to this. He lifted his glass and bowed his head to mark the moment.

"And...?" Maz pressed.

"Ah, yes, my peroration." He smacked his lips. "You are an artist, *maestro*, you blessed creature of the earth's loins, it is your lot to suck at the teats of sensuality."

This bohemian bullshit. Maz thought this line had gone out in the 1930s. But of course it would still stalk the nights, like a vampire, down here.

Leggit stood and carefully pushed his barstool aside, then leaned close to Maz' ear and said "I know the kine-a music you wanna hear."

"What?"

"My suspicion is you never heard it before," Leggit breathed. "But there always will come a time in a man's life where some inexorable something is destined. Even the things that seem like little things. Like just a little ol' music."

"What?" Again, Maz was drawn in by the man's style, delivery, even though he could barely understand the substance of what he said.

"If what you wanna hear is jazz, though, what I got in mind, this is the real dealy-deal. Distilled. You got to go to the source."

"It depends on what you call jazz."

"Indeed. Indeed." Leggit nodded vigorously. "It certainly does depend on that. But see, me, what I call jazz—and I think you'll come around—I'm talking about from the way down under gutbucket." His eyes narrowed and he lowered his voice. "Some funky-ass dick shit. Now are you game?"

Yeah, Maz was game.

A car waited outside—not a cab—with a driver who seemed not only to know Leggit, but to have been waiting for him. It was a Leggit kind of car, a late '70s Lincoln, dark but with a white leather interior *I'm white inside but what did I do*. They got in the back seat and when Maz asked Leggit about the (black) man up front, Leggit just said, "Oh, he does some work for me, y'know," and took out his cigarette case and offered Maz one. They lit up—Pall Malls.

"Good brand," Maz said.

"It's not the quality of the smoke, though, superior as it may be. It's the memories."

"*Wherever Particular People Congregate.*"

"*In Hoc Signo Vinces!*"

"You're well acquainted with the cigarette pack literature."

"Let's say I smoke them tonight in honor of you, a man who has played an indisputable role."

Maz waited for him to expand but he never did. "Did you buy me that pack at the bar?"

"Of course I did. I wanted to honor you. But what I want to know is, can you remember the taste? I mean from then, y'know back in the big days on Division Street. What it was like lighting up then, on the stage, in the light? The nicotine buzz—" He paused to admire the curling blue smoke drifting from his mouth. "Tobacco's such a fine drug. Up on stage, looking out at the fans and uttering some shtick of some kind to get 'em relaxed and primed? Do you have a memory like that? Can you recall the faces of the girls—excuse me, I mean that metaphorically—"

"I've slept with plenty of women."

"Y'know, whoever it would be, at the front-row tables. Lookin' up atcha. Y'know back when it was all just opening up … as opposed to closing in?"

"I don't remember much, actually," Maz admitted. It was true: his memory was more like a cataloged record, of responses to and interpretations of experiences, not so much a collection of faded sensations. What was the point in that? "But nothing's closing in," he asserted. "I'm on a groove."

Maz heard an electronic whir and saw the window go down and Leggit leaning his head out. A retching sound. Leggit was vomiting. The car didn't slow down and the driver didn't say anything. Then the window went back up and Leggit puffed on his cigarette—it had never left his hand—and produced a pewter flask. He politely waved it at Maz before hitting it. Maz took a hit and handed it back to him. Bourbon, of course. Or rum. Surely he wouldn't

65

have mixed the two? Then the smell of vomit and booze and cigarette smoke and something else (his own unwashed body?) pushed Maz to roll down his window. The air was lovely and he couldn't figure out why the windows were up in the first place. He saw they'd just crossed Barracks. Barracks and Rampart. This neighborhood again. They pulled to the curb about a block away from where he'd gotten mugged.

"Is this an O.K. neighborhood?" he asked, stepping out of the car as he'd been instructed. Leggit got some of his sense of humor back. He laughed low and coughed a little—didn't answer the question though. He just said, "Got Uptown, y'got Downtown. And then there's the Back o'town."

The driver stayed in the car. The white men headed toward a loud cluster of black partiers spilling out of an open door on the corner. Marijuana smoke wafted toward them, an invitation, on the Turkish, Tunisian, soft air, reminding Maz that he wanted to get high again. But Leggit seemed unaffected by it. He snorted something out of a round little antique-looking snuffbox, but didn't offer Maz any.

Almost everybody on the corner greeted Leggit with some kind of physical contact—they slapped his hand, patted his shoulder, touched his arm. But nobody touched Maz. Just eyed him suspiciously.

Until Leggit introduced him: "My friends and countrymen, I'd like y'all to meet uuhh ... a fellow enthusiast." With this they ceased all conversation among themselves and…all of them? Yes. Why? In silence they stared at Maz intently, almost soberly. But it only lasted a second. Then came an ambiguous chuckle, one nodded and one looked away, another made a sucking sound, one said, "awright then," and Leggit laughed in earnest, loud and hard, eyes undone and rolling back toward his brain, head pointed up at a muscular green and brown arm of the twisting live oak leaning over all of them.

Maz didn't know what to feel about the oak *in the southern breeze hanging from the poplar trees* but he felt confusion because of the people, because he wanted to assimilate all their faces, different faces and shapes and clothes and eyes, but he couldn't: they were just them.

But he stopped thinking about it because of what came from inside the place. The band had started up. The sounds flew in the face of confusion, any confusion. The blare soaked him to the bones from even way over where he was standing, outside and through a sea of bodies. What about right up against it? In it? What could that be like? He wandered inside and Leggit grinned at him. Followed him in grinning. Put his arm over his shoulder and said, "Well let's us belly on up to the bar."

The bartender, a large very black woman with a diamond in her nose and golden hair, called Leggit Mister Leggit. And he said, "Why dontcha call me Davis?" and she said "Whatever you say, Mister Davis." She fixed up two bourbon and sodas without being told—Maz didn't much care what the drinks were—and the music made it seem ridiculous that anything like conversation was going on at all. It was a haphazard brass ensemble, with no clear sense of organization according to balance or economy. Four trumpet players? No, a couple were cornets. One alto. A bari—no, tenor. One slide trombone, but maybe another one sitting it out. And the most important of all: TWO sousaphones positively cussing the bass-line. Maz had never heard such a sound. You couldn't say they had range. They all just blared as loud as they could—which made it miraculous when they sweated and strained enough to bump the din up a few notches whenever the head came around. One drummer on bass and one on snare, both standing and shuffling around while they played—like all the players. They all worked their feet like the crowd in front of them.

Maz wondered what was wrong with the picture and then it hit him: even though he and Leggit were the only white people in the place, no one seemed to worry about them or notice them, even, at all. No one stared. If someone happened to bump into them (plenty bumping going on), they either said 'excuse' or didn't and kept right on. Marched right on. They all kept right on marching, either in tight little circles or in broad swaths that reached every wall of the place, cutting in and out of the boiling tangle of bodies at different points like electrons must. Or water molecules.

But somebody out there **was** looking at Maz. Was staring. He felt it, but couldn't locate the eyes. Below the radar somewhere, like a cat in the reeds. Not Leggit. Leggit was talking (shouting) with the bartender, craning over the bar and pointing at bottles and shaking his head or nodding.

Maz heard him say, "You don't wanna get no European beers in here. This ain't Europe."

The bartender said, "But they good. German beer is good."

Leggit: "Forget it."

Maz finally located the face trained on his: a boy. A boy with a cornet. A boy with skin the color of a worn wet brick sidewalk, soft as the backside of a magnolia leaf. Trombone lips with edges delicate enough to swing a cornet. Yet a soft, edgeless tongue. This cat was a cheetah. The same. The cat from the Square. But in this setting, he also looked familiar from another place.

Maz stared back at him but he didn't look away like he was supposed to. It was a nonchalant look, but it wasn't exactly serene. And with the music around him, the kid seemed lifted up or larger or thrown in some kind of light that went way beyond his physical frame. It also made him seem much older and much wiser than he really could be, at his age—fourteen? Fifteen? The music backed him like an army would, like fists raised, clutching guns. And the kid nodded and set his chin and mouthed a "Dat's right" and lifted his horn to his face and stepped up to take a solo.

The fattest, most pissed-off bitching whine and growl Maz had ever heard. And he played out of the side of his mouth like he'd never had a proper lesson in his life. The root of the sound seemed to be the brassy shouting of a King Oliver or a Satch—the daemon of Buddy Bolden, who somebody said you could hear a mile away. But cut with micro-tonal ornamentation—the notes slid around like men wrestling in the mud on a slanting levee. Like Miles, but earthier. Muddy. Other ingredients were, yes, a mystery. But not a quiet mystery. A mystery like a heart-attack is a mystery: you don't stand around and ponder it, challenge it with questions, you just die.

But what was here was too hot to be death. Maz hadn't been sweating before—certainly not at the *Kozy Kove*—but now he felt the beads pushing through the layer of invisible grime that finely coats the skin on trains and in New Orleans. Like every drop of sweat wanted to get out there and boogie, too, like the people, and be joined with their brethren in a big camp meeting of the sweat of myriad bodies rapidly coming together on the floor of the place. The kid's cornet was right on the thermostat, frowning and threatening and ignoring all supplicants, sending the mercury up, up. The band started chanting "Talk Dat Shit Now!" and "Say What?!" and pointing at people on the dance floor. The boy blowing into his horn through the side of his mouth found some undiscovered and previously unused muscle in his face or his belly and started swinging and leaned into it, bumped the volume up one more decibel, and treated the air in front of his cornet to a righteous, vicious pummeling. The other cats first yelled and then came in on their horns and the kid took the solo out through the upstairs exit, some previously unknown-to-man pitch up in the sky somewhere that Maz doubted he could hit even on his soprano. The temperature on the dance floor went from Fahrenheit to Kelvin. People yelled, shrieked, and started jumping as high as they could and spinning around. And crouching low down to the ground and marching around that way. And Maz discovered that he was up and dancing too. *Feets don't fail me now*

But his groove got busted when the kid lowered his horn emphatically and spit on the floor and shot a look right at him like a bullet. Then Maz recognized him. Not from the Square. From the street. Recognized that if this kid had been in possession of a bullet that very afternoon, then Maz would have spent his evening differently, lying on the sidewalk waiting to be cleaned up by the sanitation department. Probably, anyway.

Leggit yelled, "I guess the Saints won tonight!"

"What?"

"They provide that jam whenever we win. Game at the dome tonight. Bears, I believe." He laughed soundlessly, like a dog panting from the heat, and his eyes did their thing. Yes, Leggit was a dog all right. Ridiculous in suit and hat, drink at his side. All he needed was floppy ears, a deck of cards, and some well-dressed dog companions.

The band had decided to mercy the feet and work the hips instead, played a blues ballad— "Back O'Town Blues." It was the only down-tempo number they did the whole night. And even it seemed antsy, jerky, not smooth, not rich like a ballad should be. They rushed it, always jumped the beat. They couldn't let it find peace, had to keep kicking it whenever it wanted to sigh.

Right before they breaked again (how many sets did

they plan to do?) the kid with the cornet stepped up and did a vocal of "How Come My Dog Don't Bark When You Come Around?" A vicious revenge murder ballad. New Orleans had produced a wealth of that stuff. Full of cutting, shooting. A celebration of righteous, joyful hatred.

And the boy—the cheetah or the snake, the cornetist—glared right at Maz through much of it. Maz stood flinty in the face of his harsh treatment, though. The music made it easier. The boy's hostility was couched in the horn. Maz could pretend it wasn't what it was. He stared right back, and listened.

Leggit noticed. He made a sucking sound with his tongue and leaned and mumbled in Maz' ear. Maz heard sharp, unbelievable words. *Wanna whip him?*

"What?" he said. "What did you say?"

"Wanna whippet? They got 'em here."

"What's a whippet?"

"Nitrous oxide. It's legal in this state."

Leggit moved down the bar and halfway behind it and spoke with the bartender. He called her Berta. Could that be her name, too? Yes, she wore a big gold pendant that spelled it out. And she called him Davis, with no "Mister." They clucked and chuckled and glanced back not too subtly at Maz. Then Leggit waved him over and Berta the barmaid unlocked a narrow door and in the two men went.

A ratty low couch in a small room, a little lamp with red tassels, and two women sitting on the couch. Yep, hookers, definitely. One of them seemed white at first, but then Maz decided she was just light-skinned. He looked them over out of some knee-jerk instinct and Leggit watched him do it with a little probing smirk on his face.

Maz had dated women, mainly in his youth. He was thoroughly capable of having sex with them, but they just didn't interest him emotionally or intellectually. Too often they seemed to be seeking out dependence. A two-sided dependence, sure, but still, the women in Maz's life seemed too quick to scuttle his and their own autonomy in the name of "love," "relationship," "commitment," whatever. Too clingy, too close. Personalizing everything. Unprofessional. Sticky. Sure, Maz had known guys like that too—but not for long.

But Maz leered at the hookers because he felt almost duty-bound to do it. That was their purpose, their function, their art. After a few pregnant seconds, Leggit said, "Ev'nin' girls, we just want to sit with y'all for a minute." They nodded and smirked just as cutely as Leggit did—but in a black way—and one of them moved over to make room on the couch. Leggit offered the spot to Maz and Maz sat down.

The whippet looked appetizing. Because Maz's skin was hot to the touch, he had run out of sweat, and the way the balloon stretched and swallowed the freezing gas and how the cold steam wafted up from it—like a ticket to the place where they make Coca Cola commercials all the day long.

He had seen the contraption before, on the Bourbon Street sidewalk. They were charging a dollar a hit, within feet of consenting policemen, in front of a Daiquiri place. He'd watched a middle-aged Midwestern housewife take one and collapse in the Bourbon Street gutter—quite possibly the filthiest gutter in America. He'd been disgusted then, but now he was ready, ripe for a collapse of his own. It had been too long since he had fallen in a gutter. In fact, he may never have.

He sucked up the contents of the balloon and died. In a cold off-blue throb. A mist of windblown snow off frozen Lake Michigan. Then a pulsing heat like the earth's core. But the best thing about the trip was how short it was. He came throbbing back and felt the normal again—normal drunk—but just not as stifling as it had felt before.

"What a thing to do," Maz muttered, as soon as he was able.

"Yass," Leggit grinned, his eyes closed. "Big with the kids these days. So who said we too old to learn new tricks from the young'uns, eh, dog?" Now his laugh came out low, deep, steady, like something with no beginning or end, like groundwater.

On Leggit's suggestion, they "moseyed" back out to the bar, where Leggit conducted some businessy-looking chatter with the band members—but not with the cheetah, or mugging punk, or whatever he was. The one who'd caught Maz's eye and squeezed. That one sat off alone, chatting with a passel of girls.

Maz wandered outside and drank up the eminently drinkable air. He attached himself to a group of stoners, saying, "Could I get a hit off that?" They let him in. He said it tasted good and one of them said, "Yeah-you-right," but didn't really look at him. None of them really did. Until he started to turn away and one of them said, "Watch dat back."

Maz faced him and said, "What?" and the man replied, point-blank, in his eyes, "You on the front now. You best go find yo' friend and grab on his pantses."

Restrained but real laughter arose from the other men. Maz just said, "Thanks for the hit," and went back inside.

He found Leggit but didn't grab his pants-leg. He just said, "What's up?"

Leggit placed his hand on Maz's shoulder in a solemn gesture, right up by the neck, and said, "Boy, we need to get you home."

"Chicago?"

"Well, maybe you had better sleep something off a little bit and think about gettin' you back to Chicago some other day." Leggit laughed, but without much energy. Maz laughed, too, he figured what the hell.

They walked back to the car and Maz said, "So that's the new marching band sounds, huh?"

Leggit: "But, of course, the new marching band sounds are not really new, not really, it's the same old thing in different clothes."

Maz asked him about the star cornetist.

Leggit told him to stay away from that one, said he had a problem with white people.

"I dig it," Maz said.

"Dig what?"

"Well, I do dig that music, too, y'know. Y'know I'm not really sure if I'll go back to Chicago at all. Seems like a nice enough place to retire."

"Yes," Leggit agreed, "that's why those that never leave here begin their life with retirement."

Leggit seemed never to retire from merriment. Maz doubted he could live that way.

"Besides," Leggit continued, "you should stay at least… indefinitely. We've been expecting you for so long."

"Expecting me?"

"Oh, well, certainly."

"Why didn't I hear about it?"

"There's ways to get a message across and also there's ways a message doesn't get received."

"What?"

"Let's us just say there are many gods, my most reverend Maz, and therefore many who haven't consented to be dead as much as the big Christian daddy has."

Maz just shook his head and said, "Oh, stop with that kind of talk, I'm too old for that."

"I thought you wanted to be young again."

"Who told you that?"

"Maybe I smelt it."

"Oh, stop with that."

They let him off at the corner of Barracks and Dauphine—a block from his guest house. A couple of shapes crawled over the iron gate of Cabrini Park and began shadowing him. But he made it to his guest house before they could accost him.

In the comfort of his private room, his loge, a cool breeze found him. Wandered through the window for some reason and enveloped him. He stripped off the sheets and lay there naked and accepted the air's attentions. Let it put his heart to rest and his mind at ease and his body to sleep.

SIDE B

III. HOW DEEP IS THE OCEAN 🎺 MODERATE, RELAXED

How much do I love you?
I'll tell you no lie
How deep is the ocean?
How high is the sky?
—as sung by Doc Cheatham, at the *Bourbon Street Jazzclub*, Amsterdam, October 28, 1957.

Maz woke to the horn of a distant train and the hubbub of birds on the patio. He dressed and descended. His host, Wendell, sat at one of the cast-iron tables on the shady patio. Wendell dressed like a banker on his day off. Crested polos tucked into khaki shorts. Loafers. He asked Maz if he wanted coffee. Yes. Here, under the crape myrtles.

The next hour or so he whiled away in the presence of the bronze fountain youth. He was quite a hottie, as the kids put it. But the sculptor had been tasteful enough to cover the lad's genitalia. He wore what looked like an Egyptian-style loincloth, textured like linen. The garment was made to hug the statue's exquisite posterior in a lifelike way, as if wet. Each round cheek was well defined. The sound of the water and the sight of it, trickling down the upraised arm and over the shoulder, down back and front, lulled Maz into a velvety blankness. He felt no urge to do anything. And that was fine.

Eventually he got up and hit the streets of the Quarter for some aimless meandering. Stopped in at a café for breakfast.

Lingered there, too. Read in the local paper that the public schools planned to put the kids in uniforms. Waiter and maid uniforms would be the most appropriate. Somehow the idea of New Orleans and the idea of uniforms didn't gel together in his mind, but, hell, it was their city. They just wanted to be Americans, after all. Suckers. They could use some lessons in efficiency, though, no doubt. Maz had to wait fifteen minutes to get his check. Good thing he was in a waiting mood.

Recalling his late urge to get a beret, he set himself the mild task of obtaining one. He'd pick up some music paper, too. That way he could mix in some light productivity—the string arrangements for his new ballad album—with the sublime pleasures of idleness, which he had never felt as sublimely as he did now. A stoned feeling. A luxuriant vagueness rested within. He had indeed decided to stay on "indefinitely." That's what he'd told Berta. He realized now that he meant it. Indefinitely—it had such a promising ring to it. Good things came to those willing to suspend urgency. If you could let life flow by, life would flow by. Chicago people didn't seem to get that. Even when they "relaxed," they did so in structured ways, in designated places. The ball park, the mall, gym. Sure, the jazz club, too. Special places reserved for ordained R 'n R at the proper times. That was him, he knew. But he didn't want to be that way anymore.

The customary wind chimes and calliope accompanied his stroll to the French Market. The sights contributed to Maz' rare sense of contentment. Ornate galleries brimming with plants and billowing colored fabrics. Hand-holding lovers everywhere. The waiters and kitchen staffs smoking on the narrow sidewalks, made even narrower by the trucks unloading boxes of produce, or antiques, or cases, cases, cases of beer. Smiles and greetings for everyone. A world without conflict. *What a wonderful world.* Everybody seemed happy. And that's what Maz felt—happy. How unassuming and deceptively easy the mood was. It just came to one *love makes me treat you the way that I do.*

Maz had decided to let his hair grow long. He'd been fighting it all his life. In his activist days he'd been especially careful to keep it short—clean-cut, even, by '60s and '70s standards. No sideburns, moustache, nothing. He ducked into a little shop with an array of old mirrors lining the walls, to look at himself. Gray stubble had formed on his cheeks, which seemed sunken to him. He looked good, though, earthy. He'd always been a compulsive shaver. But that, too, was past. He was becoming a different man. He pulled his hair back to see if enough strands could be pulled together to merit a pony-tail. Possibly. He looked for an attendant to borrow a rubber-band from, but there was no one. The back door of the long narrow room opened onto a patio. Secret gardens everywhere, around here. Possibly the proprietor was back there. Besides mirrors—of different sizes and frames, but all old, weathered, blotched—the store was cramped with bureaus, dressers, trunks. They all looked heavy and not in the best condition. Dust coated everything, too, and suffused the air. A moldy smell, too. He called out a 'hello' but got no answer. Whatever.

As he was leaving, he stumbled on an open trunk. It contained a human skeleton. It was clean, though, bleached, and neatly folded in three layers, the skull propped against the edge comfortably, like someone lounging in a bathtub. The messy, sick, treacherous flesh boiled away, the eternal form shone. In flawless handwriting, an attached tag announced, "Complete Skeleton of 8 year-old girl. $800."

Maz stepped out again into the sun. Pale blue sky, lazy wisps of clouds, seventy degrees. Bright banners waved in the breeze at the French Market. He couldn't find a beret, though, strangely enough. He considered getting a straw hat—they had quite a variety—but he was too worried about looking like Leggit. He settled on something like a beret: one of those knit things Rastafarians wear over their dreds. The bright tie-dye colors seemed to go well with the sun and sky and the paint on the buildings.

He'd planned to pick up staff paper at one of his very favorite music stores—an old-fashioned multi-story music department store on Canal Street. The slow economy of New Orleans meant throwback places like this survived years after they bit the dust in other parts of America. He hopped the Vieux Carré bus to get there—a "mini-bus," shaped like a streetcar. Even a few riders made it seem crowded.

It was lucky for Maz he wasn't the only passenger, because the driver needed assistance. Apparently he wasn't sure about the route. After a wrong turn, the riders cheerfully corrected him. It happened a few times.

"Then you go clear up to Poland on Chartres, *then* you hang the left."

"Naw, naw, you turn the left on Press Street, by the tracks, then you head down on Dauphine."

"At least I can drive!" The driver laughed.

And they all laughed with him. Maz, too. Apparently no one was in a hurry. That was the key.

Maz's disappointment came on Canal Street, when he finally got off the bus and saw that his favorite music store *had* finally bit the dust. It was now a boutique hotel. He stood there wondering what to do. Looked at the city signage up and down the boulevard: "Re-build New Orleans Now!" Apparently this meant hotels instead of music stores.

An old fat white man, sitting in a folding chair on the sidewalk, had been observing him. "You lookin' for de Werlein's?" he said. He wore one of those Cubano shirts so common here, fanned himself with the coupon section from the paper. "Dey got a brand new one, a big one, out in Metry. You got to go to Metry."

Maz wasn't familiar with the neighborhood. "Can you get there on a bus?" Maz asked.

"Not unless you got a couple o'days," haw-hawed the man. "It's way out dere, by de airport."

A black woman dressed like a secretary had approached and taken interest in Maz's plight. "Dey got one in de Quarters now."

"No, dey ain't," said the white man.

85

"They do, though, right by the new House O'Blues."

The old white man just repeated, "no, dey ain't." The black woman sent Maz around the corner to the left, where he found the new Werlein's.

It was in no way comparable to the old one. More like a record store. Not much sheet music, not many instruments. No pianos or organs. Plenty of New Orleans T-shirts, though. He asked the man behind the counter for music paper.

"What?" He stared at Maz in utter confusion.

"Y'know, music paper. Staff paper. To write music on."

"I don't know," he said, and surveyed the store lazily. He then appeared to return to his reading. Maz wondered if it was an inventory list or something. He leaned over and saw it was a car magazine.

"So…" Maz ventured. "You think y'all have any music paper?"

He looked up again. Appeared to give the issue some thought. "I don't know," he said. "Maybe in the back." He waved his hand at the back of the store and returned to his car magazine.

Maz stood there a second longer and then wandered to the back. They did have music paper. Plenty of it. Maz picked up a spiral notebook but realized he was clean out of cash. He hated to put such a small charge on a credit card. Some places had minimum purchase requirements and he didn't want to just keep adding stuff to get up to twenty bucks or whatever. Acting on a sudden whim, he stuck the notebook in the back of his pants. He returned to the counter and asked the guy if they sold pens. He didn't think so. Did he have one Maz could borrow? Sure. Maz took the pen and left the store.

He made his way to the Square. Maybe the cheetah would be there and Maz could peer at him from a safe distance while toying with his arrangements. He bought a daiquiri for the hell of it, a bright green one (with a credit card), and positioned himself on an iron bench within the Square, but with an easy view through the fence to the front of the Presbytere. The Cabildo spot was taken by jugglers and fire-eaters, so if the band came, they'd have to come here. He was sure they'd come. Good things came to those who sat on benches with daiquiris in New Orleans. *Fetch me that Gin, son, fo' I tan yo'…*

Soon enough a brass band showed up, set out the bucket, and stood there talking, occasionally blowing a warm-up note or two. Maz couldn't tell if they were the same cats from yesterday. No cheetah. No white guy, either. Maz wondered what he'd do if Leggit sauntered up. He couldn't picture him out in the sun like this. Then he wondered what he'd do if his sax were here. Why *didn't* he have his axe? Surely he could get out to "Metry" or wherever and buy a decent one. Or have one sent down.

Better yet, he could buy a used one, an indigenous one, a haunted one, at one of these dusty shops tucked in a Quarter backstreet. Yes. He'd decided. Get an instrument, stupid. Sit in with the young cats. On the street, whatever.

Nobody knew who he was (not the Americans, anyway). He was a new man. A stranger who suddenly showed up on the streets of New Orleans with a saxophone. If people asked, he'd say he just walked up out of the river.

Not today, though. Tomorrow, maybe. Or the day after. What a thrill: to know he had a future yet in no hurry to get there. He hummed lightly while he sketched in clefs, time signatures. *On a slow boat to China*…that's where he was… *with you*

No cheetah yet. The band had started up, though. Did *Closer Walk With Thee*. Swung into *Didn't He Ramble*. They were all right. Couldn't put them with strings, though. You needed refinement for that. Needed some cool. Some training. In harmony, especially. Not too much, though, or it wouldn't be jazz anymore. He had to walk that line, and these young black cats didn't have to worry about that. But the art was in the cool, he'd always maintained, the hot was really just a form of folk music. Not that he hadn't been taken to task for such views. But he still believed it—the raw stuff had to be taken in hand, had to be disciplined, to attain the level of art. Maz's critics never gave him that much credit. They carped about "imitation" but what they failed to realize is that the process of imitation involved all kinds of formal maneuvering that eventually elevated the material into a different, unique species. Less vernacular, sure. So? What the fuck was wrong with refinement? It kept us from rooting around in the mud and smelling each others' crotches, didn't it? His job was to cool the hot, which involved higher intellectual functions, some application of form. People like Amiri Baraka saw white musicians approaching black music consciously, studying it like a problem with possibilities, and pronounced it theft, and nostalgia. Another guy said on the radio once—a New Orleans cat, in fact—that black people make music in the present, and that's why they keep coining new musical languages. But why always leave everything behind? Maz knew the Johnny-Come-Lately to a music form was able to apply nostalgia like a formal principle—and thereby change the character of the music in the process. So it was a paler shade of blue. So? A pretty nice color. A cool shade.

The band in front of the Presbytere traded in nostalgia like a racket, though. For the tourists. That's why they played that way. Nothing like the nasty writhing they boiled up last night. Actually, at least one of the players—the bass-drum—*was* in the band last night. Possibly the trombone, too. It was hard to tell because, even if they were the same guys, they *weren't* the same musicians. It wasn't even the same planet. Honestly, Maz didn't know which he liked better.

Is that what he was here to find out?

He was glad he didn't have to choose. It was day, after all, and before, that was a thing of the night. Duplicitous like the night, too. It kissed you, roughly, but did it really like you? Maz wondered what the night had in store for him. He shuddered—not without pleasure—and was glad it was still day. Luckily, the sun in this place knew how exacting the night was, so he gave you lots of time to recover.

Sympathized.

But Maz knew he'd be ready, when night fell. He couldn't be in New Orleans and not go out. He'd meet it head on. He'd jump in and swim *smack dab in the middle*. He scribbled the word "indefinitely" at the top of the staff. Great name for a ballad. He softly sang a rising line of five notes, "*Till death* (beat, beat) *do us part*."

And then came the call. The cheetah call. He had arrived. Maz kept his eyes down and listened, didn't want to look yet. A very bright, brassy rendition of *I Cover the Waterfront*. Upbeat. "*I'm watching the sea*," Maz crooned, but softly. This boy, too, seemed different than the one wearing the same skin the night before. His solo over, Maz looked up and saw him smile big and bow for the handful of slow gathering fans. A sunny, utterly unselfconscious smile. But it couldn't possibly be real. He then ambled off, in his sure, unified, unhurried gait, to a spot apart. And stood, evenly spraddled, like a fine assassin at ease, and gently nodded his chin in time to his compatriots' music.

Today he wore black slacks. They seemed like standard waiter issue, by far the most common trouser type in the Quarter. And a loose billowing Hawaiian shirt with great green leaves and red flowers. He wore shades, today, too. Maz had seen the style at the French Market. Long horizontal rectangles, a greenish shade of brown. The boy's hands were broad, and well-proportioned with his forearms. One gripped and the other fluttered fingers over the keys.

Maz indulged himself, imagining conversations with

him. "Oh, you're Maz Mazewski?" the boy would say. Maz would smile back, "Yes." Maz would be gracious as the boy confessed his great appreciation. Maz would agree to give him lessons in harmony, arranging. They would develop a beautiful, musically significant relationship. Maz became comfortable with an image of the cheetah's face close to his own, wearing an expression of respect, attentiveness, affection.

Maz's contentment soon took the form of drowsiness. The daiquiri, maybe. Or last night catching up to him. He found himself nodding off. Soft voices came to him in fragments of dreams, but he couldn't identify speakers, or remember what they said, besides his name. It didn't matter, because the little pieces of speech blended into such a sweet, benevolent tone. He considered whether he should go curl up on the grass and pass out—he wouldn't be the only one. But he couldn't bring himself to such a step. Not that far gone, yet. He decided instead to scrape up whatever last dregs of leftover initiative he had and walk—slowly—back to his room, where he could nap in private, store up strength for the inevitable big night.

He wasn't sure if he had ever felt as sleepy as he did now. He exited the Square on a side far from the band—he just wasn't ready to pass so close—and shuffled like a zombie toward his guest house. The lovely sights, sounds, and smells now had a pleasantly muffled character, as if taken in from under sheets and pillows. He did his best to maintain the feeling, like someone, not ready to rise yet, who takes care of some morning business with only one eye slightly open. He bumped into a couple of people, but they didn't seem to mind. His clumsiness drew no nasty upbraidings, as he was sure would have happened in Chicago.

The nearer he approached his guest house, the more he allowed tendrils of sleep to overtake this or that part of him. He was returning home to a lover. But not for sex. *But not for me.* The innocent, inquisitive face of the cheetah, nestled in his mind, awaited his pillows. Yes. But not for sex. Nothing that vulgar. For sleep. Sleep would unleash the dream, and here, here only, they could be whole together.

But his private date was rudely postponed. By a sudden blow to the back of the head. He heard the hollow sound of a board striking his skull before he felt the pain. He collapsed onto his hands and knees and took a kick to his liver. He fell on his side and curled up tight, covering his head in his arms. His attacker had words for him, too. "*Get up, bitch.*" The words were low in volume, high in pitch, and loaded with venom. Two arms forcibly snaked under his own and pulled him upright in a full nelson. He opened his eyes but kept them pointed at the sidewalk. There he saw the offending instrument: an old weather-board ripped off of some rotting house. He didn't dare look at his attackers. There seemed to be two. To look them in the eye would have devastating consequences, possibly for his body, definitely for his mind, heart. He tried hard to keep his eyes off the face commanding the hands that plundered his pockets. That way he could pretend there was no face. Just hands. It was hands that would do such a thing. A face would make it impossible.

The hands, attached to arms, came in two sets: one black, one brown. He saw only the forearms of one, craning from behind him, gripping him like two fragments of a single, whole anaconda. The other set of hands worked quickly, rifling his pockets. He saw the legs, too. Skinny, dirty, bruised legs, in old ratty shorts. These thugs were filthy and smelled it. He much preferred yesterday's muggers. He suddenly wished these men had a gun. The gun simplified robbery, made it more humane, turned it into a gentlemanly agreement. These men, on the other hand, were hungry, angry. Savages. Speech would be lost on them. Maz didn't ask to keep his credit cards this time, didn't say anything. A big brown fist popped him in the face, anyway. It caused a dark red flash to ripple through his insides, made him lurch like vomiting. The one in back shoved him to the ground again and Maz found he was content to lie there. He heard another "*Bitch!*" as they walked off.

Maz rolled onto his back and lay on the sidewalk for a while. Breathed a bit. The pain subsided. The dull thud in his head and neck faded away. He opened his eyes and looked at the sky. Broad daylight.

The sun had betrayed him. It didn't even care. How could all those happy people he'd seen all day live the lie they obviously lived? Or was it all a performance, all rigged to put people like him at ease so they'd be easy pickings?

His guest house wasn't far. In fact, it was right in front of him. But the black bastards had taken his key. Maz rang the bell and Wendell opened the door with a big hearty "Hi!" He then asked Maz if he'd been having a nice day.

"Sorry I don't have my key," Maz said.

"Did you leave it in your room?"

"No, I took it with me."

"Oh, dear. Well, don't worry, honey, we've got extra."

"I got mugged." His lip felt warm and buzzed with sensation. He looked in a mirror and saw it had started to swell.

"Oh my God!" Wendell emoted. "That's terrible!" It sounded too rehearsed to Maz.

"Are you all right? Do you want to call the police?"

Maz said no, but didn't like the too-evident look of relief on his host's face.

"Where did this happen?" He looked worried again.

"Right out front, as a matter of fact." Maz tried to laugh, to show he didn't think assault was that big a deal, but only a grunt came out. So he said, "This kind of thing happen often?"

Wendell considered the question too long, then stuttered out, "Well, there is a crime rate… "

Maz had to smile at that.

"… but usually not—not that often, anyway—in this neighborhood. Not right around here. And you know, sometimes there are sudden flare-ups and then it just goes away."

Maz must have looked unsatisfied with this because

Wendell capped off his explanation with the perfect sigh. "You know, it's drugs." The only other thing he had to say was "go figure." Maz just walked off, shaking his head. Wendell told him to wait, gave him another key, and Maz headed upstairs.

He ascended in a state of bewilderment. He couldn't figure out the purpose of the experience. What was the cosmos trying to tell him? That it didn't like him? He still managed to sleep, but the sleep was fitful, broken. The dreams weren't the blissful ones he'd ordered so carefully. The cheetah's face was gone. Worse: it was attached to the body of an anaconda, baring teeth. Bad acid. The sun and the cheetah, and Davis Leggit, all joined hands and laughed together at the spectacle of Maz, on the sidewalk, outside. Behold and laugh: a man not in the know, a permanent outsider, stupidly crashing a party where he knew he was hated.

IV. WHAT IS THIS THING CALLED LOVE 🎺 VERY FAST♪

Why?

Should it make a fool of me?

—as sung by Anita O'Day, April 19, 1958, at *The Famous Door*, New Orleans.

Morning? Afternoon? All Maz saw was Anita O'Day's face wide-open and laughing, head thrown back—always so bubbly. A cynical laugh, though, disarming only to stab. And Teagarden's face ... not laughing. Just staring soberly, hungover rancid soberly, head shaking. Bulging sunken bloodshot eyes right in Maz's, saying shame, shame and it's too late now. Drawn face like he hadn't slept a wink since his death *cover the waterfront I'm watching the sea*. Mr. Tall Dark and Handsome. Not anymore. Where was he calling from? Maz ripped himself away and picked up the phone. It was warm from the bright sunlight flooding the window. East? West? Afternoon?

A voice told him someone named "Berta Bredaux" was on the line. Did he want to talk to her?

Maz mumbled an OK, wondering where he was.

"Maz! You never told me where you were staying!"

"Berta ... shit. I'm trying to stay afloat."

"What?"

Maz strained and burst himself through the surface, forced Big T.'s face under and forgot it. Anita went, too.

"I'm sorry. You taking a nap?"

"Yeah. No, just sleeping."

"I was too. Had a weird dream about you and ... I don't know. I wanted to see if you were O.K."

Maz said, yeah, sure, and what time was it?

Afternoon, late—evening, really.

"You went carousing around with that Leggit, didn't you?"

"Uh-huh. He's a fun guy. A little crazy."

"Yes, a little crazy."

"You dream about him?"

"Not him directly."

Maz told her to hold on and went to the window to lean his head out, in search of a vague memory of cool water in the air. But the breeze had warmed up too much. It kept him groggy. But a pleasant groggy, so he didn't really care. He picked up the phone and asked her to repeat whatever she'd said.

Berta paused so long Maz thought maybe she'd gone away, but then: "First it was me playing, you know, in some club—looked a little like the *Kove*, but it wasn't supposed to be. Then I was in the audience and it was this other pianist—a woman, white woman. And we had this kind of conversation going, too, y'know, while all this was going on. Then I saw her walking around ... naked ... over in Tremé, I think, or some other pretty ghetto 'hood, y'know? And these cats were with her. I mean felines, walking along with her and crawling up and down on her. Cats. Toms. Strays, feral. Well, it didn't

97

come to me who she was until after I woke up and then it just flashed at me but ... it's not like it's somebody I ever cared about or liked their music or ever even thought about? ... Norma Teagarden."

"Jack Teagarden's sister? Well, she did play, right? Piano?"

"Yeah ..."

"I don't know if she ever recorded anything-"

"I did see her once, though, *once*—in San Francisco *years* ago. '60s, musta been."

"Well, y'know," Maz stammered. He couldn't bring himself to care about Berta's dreams. "The strangest things come to you ... So what does that have to do with me?"

"Mmm, it's 'cause of Leggit, who you should definitely not be out there prowling around with."

"He's fun."

"A lot of stuff is fun, Maz."

"What's the connection though? Did he show up in the dream too?"

"The only reason I can think of that I would dream of Norma Teagarden—besides, y'know, the fact that you can't really read dreams, anyway—is 'cause of Leggit 'Cause back then he had this strange episode with her."

"Really?"

Berta said back then in San Fran was when she'd first met Leggit—somebody knew they were both from New Orleans, and (there was also that white thing back then about let's get our white and black friends together) and the whole reason Leggit was in town was to court—stalk, really—the much, much older and oblivious Norma Teagarden. She remembered the whole thing as weird and embarrassing.

Maz didn't have a response. He shrugged his shoulders but Berta couldn't hear that. She wanted to know if he'd come see her tonight. Where? *Stagolee's*, a touristy new riverfront development place, but would he please come? He said sure and hung up.

And noticed he was hard.

The humid breeze must have done it. Warmed and swollen his pecker. For the first time in years he paused and admired its form. It had a fat hungry look, a pig looking for mud to snout around in. He gripped the package at its base and squeezed and patted and rubbed and looked. He considered masturbating and letting the cum fly out the window to the crumbly soft brown bricks of the patio, maybe even hit the fountain, the bronze boy.

But he couldn't. He got dressed (same clothes).

He patted the empty space in his back-pocket and remembered his recent mugging. It pissed him off. He had money in the bank and it pissed him off that it would be such an inconvenience now to get to it. How could New Orleanians deal with the constant obstacles? Everywhere you stepped was a turtle or a slug or a roach or a snake. A town out of control, an affront to any and all citizens who stupidly make an effort to give a damn.

And the air, when he got outside, the air that earlier had been so sweet to him, now wielded a grudge. The more he breathed the worse it got. Finally he began to feel it for what it was: an unbreathable concoction of baser animal smells, cut rudely with a dose of chemical toxins—a cigarette butt floating in flat, cheap beer. And the whole mixture crammed down the faces and throats of the people by a leaden cloud cover *open up that window, let that bad air out*

His brain began to throb. It hadn't been a dream. They *had* clocked him on the back of the head. The bastards. They knocked out his lights. The sky knew it, too. That's why it had fled in shame behind the clouds. The once glorious sun was now little more than a whiter swab on the general gray.

And then the people. He'd barely walked ten yards when yet another shabby black man approached him out of nowhere. Slug or turtle or snake? Damn, they came out of the woodwork here. Festering termites.

The man wanted money—big surprise—but at least he was asking. Maz didn't know whether he respected him more or less for not just taking. He said, "Y'know, I really don't have any money."

But the pan-handler wouldn't drop it. He walked alongside Maz in a nervous bouncy stride and whined, c'mon, please please please. Some bricks had fallen from the dilapidated wall of Cabrini Park. Maz was only mildly shocked to realize how much he enjoyed the image of brutally smashing the homeless man in the face with one of them. His next thought: he knew, the cops wouldn't trouble him too much about it.

He leaned down to pick up a brick and the bum bumped into him. He weighed the brick in his hand and the homeless guy bobbed his head in fear, confusion, and mumbled, "Hey, now, hey, now," senselessly. He had crumbs of grass and dirt in his nappy hair and beard. His abundant lips lost melanin where they came together, so that an uneven line of pink, breaking up into pink and red and white splotching, sat in the middle of his face. The derisive spit of his Creator. Ugly motherfucker.

Maz clenched his teeth and said, just loud enough to barely be heard, "What you people need is discipline."

The man backed off a little ways and jumped the gate into Cabrini Park, where he retreated to an area strewn with old crates and old clothing and (sleeping?) bodies. And the ever present cats.

As per usual, Maz thought about the purpose of the experience, and, again, couldn't find one. Forced reflection didn't bear fruit, he knew. Rote, tired. Like his own self that he couldn't figure out how to change. Couldn't find a new way of living. A voice in his head said he should just accept himself. But he gave it the finger.

He stopped to get a coffee to go and saw on a *New York Times* front page a story about New Orleans: about a whole family of nice German tourists named Schlackenfluss, gunned down in Saint Roch cemetery. The reporter noted that Saint Roch was allegedly the patron saint of "miraculous cures."

They handed him his coffee and he sipped out of it, decided to put cream and sugar in it for the first time in decades, and remembered he didn't have any money. Well, he had plenty of money, just none on him. He began to stutter out an explanation, but the counter person—an Asian woman with a French accent—waved it off disgustedly, spitting out, "You go. You just go."

He went—with his coffee. He felt a small triumph about it, but it was soon swallowed up by the memory of the headline he'd just read: "Germany, U.K. Issue Travel Advisories For U.S." And then the air got to him again, unwholesome, stinging his sinuses like stomped-on cocaine.

When he got to the American Express office at Royal and Toulouse, where he'd planned to order a new card and get a cash advance, he got plane tickets instead. A train wouldn't be fast enough. He questioned the clerk about the crime situation. The guy, a white guy from New York, said the distinctive feature of New Orleans crime was "extra added hate." He said he'd been set on leaving for years, but somehow he just kept staying on.

"Not me," Maz said.

Maz guessed all the professional people in New Orleans came from somewhere else. They had to import efficiency. Their export was talent. If the cheetah was really good enough, he'd be in Chi within a year begging to blow on Maz's next album.

And there, as if pre-ordained, idled a cab outside the Amex office, more than willing to cart him to the airport. He didn't care how long he'd have to sit around waiting for his flight. It would be air-conditioned. An insulated controlled environment. Airports were reliable that way, the same, like every other outpost of the U.S. Hamburger Empire, down to the tiniest details all around the globe. Even New Orleans couldn't stand up against it: the world would all be the same one day. One giant airport. It surprised Maz to realize he felt comforted by this.

He was further relieved to note that his cabdriver was white.

"Got any bags?"

"Uh, no. No."

They pulled away from the curb and stopped and started down Toulouse, fitfully, tourists blocking the way at every step. Especially the river of bodies coursing down Bourbon like the Big Muddy itself, bumping mindlessly into each other like blood cells gushing out of a severed artery, not seeing the inevitable destination: the Gulf, a red pool on a buckled sidewalk.

The cab nudged and shoved its way through, reached the other side.

Maz said, "None of these dolts know what's going on."

No response from the man behind the wheel. Maz wondered what his face looked like. He'd never bothered to notice. He was done paying attention in this class. But when they got to Rampart the driver made a wrong turn—or at least not the turn Maz expected. He turned downtown, toward Armstrong Park, Congo Square. Maz, again, inquired about the route. He'd gotten used to pushing, micro-supervising every little task.

"Gotta get to a service station," the cabbie drawled. "She's actin' up. Might have to order you another cab." All that stopping and starting in the Quarter had gotten the engine

103

racing. Maz could see steam now, pouring out from under the hood. The cab sputtered into a gas station that seemed also to sell seafood—crudely taped to the smudged dull stucco were hand-scrawled signs advertising po-boys, crawfish. The car halted.

Maz said, "You realize this is a town where even the cabs don't work?"

The cabbie said, "Yeah, I realize that."

"And the mechanics who are supposed to maintain them and the cops who are supposed to police them? Why aren't they doing their job?"

"Beats me, mister."

"New Orleans is a disaster. It's the Big Queasy."

"You oughta leave town then. Just it won't be in mah cab." He was turned around now so Maz saw his face. Weak chin, the kind that just melts into the neck. He tried to cover it up with a trimmed beard, but the thin brown hair on the mottled purplish neck folds was worse than lipstick on a pig.

Maz shook his head and got out. He patted his pockets for cigarettes and heard…music. Bells, shakers, drums. Drifting over from the green clouds of oaks and magnolias on Congo Square. Maz bummed a cigarette off the driver and asked him about the sounds.

"Oh yeah. Snakedance dey call it. Some freaky shit, you ask me. Dey had it on the news."

A voodoo group had gotten permission to do some rituals to combat the crime wave. The cab driver kept rattling on about it but Maz drifted downstream toward the sounds. He crossed Rampart. Big crowd, cops standing around looking bored. Drummers on Congo Square. Maz didn't exactly want to see or hear them, but he thought he should. So he pressed through the crowd anyway.

The sounds discombobulated him. Made him afraid. The drums were after him. He was their quarry, and they were relentless. He felt rawhide biting into the ankle of his soul and snaring him, flattening him, face down hard in the dust. He wanted to run. But he stood transfixed. There were a few white people in the crowd, some with cameras, but they were like spray skimmed off the brown water by the cool breeze that was now blowing. Maz couldn't see the drummers but his mind rapidly formed disturbing pictures of them. The mbiras came on like deceptively gentle monsoon breezes, that stroked you while planning to level your house. The shakers and gourd rattles were too much like blood swishing through a brain at dangerously high pressure. The dun-dun didn't talk, it struck. Black fists, struck like a smart boxer: the head, then the ribs, a left to the gut, then the head again.

The djembe strafed. The bass conga was, of course, a smiling crocodile, lying in wait on a reedy, marshy riverbank.

His nauseous reverie was cut short by a youngish black woman who bumped into him, then scowled and darted away dramatically. "Mmm, somebody need to tell him 'bout deodorant, sheee!" Covering her face with her hand.

She was talking about him. That's OK, he didn't want to be there, either. He strained and worked to move himself away. But first he got a glimpse of the priestess, in full possession, on her knees and bending over backwards, being taken by Ogun or Shango or somebody. She was white. High pink, in fact. The hair that mingled with the dust from where she bent all the way back was blonde. The eyes, rolling around in a seizure, were brightest blue.

And something watched him. He felt it on his neck, where you're supposed to feel it, a tickling back of his neck. But the watcher stood right in front of him, coming in and out of view like a copper penny in shallow rippling water, through the shifting crowd and dust and heat-haze. A cheetah at the river's edge. The boy (punk? boy?) who'd watched him last night, who yesterday afternoon had craned his neck to tease him with hatred in a kiss where lips never met, trombone lips that had chosen cornet instead. Who today had declined Maz' offer to meet him in a dream of mutual respect.

Maz ran. Another dun-dun came in, from a lower register, and the two talkers dueled and fought it out and agreed and came after Maz, in synchronized foot-falls. He stumbled (or did someone trip him?) and went down and scraped up his knee. And he saw it: his blood on a sidewalk. A single black face noticed him slowly lift himself, one that Maz didn't think he'd seen before, the almond-shaped eyes came out of the gurgling brown current and assessed him and released him and sank back under. Maz rose and started off again and a kudu horn floated out above the air like the moan of a wounded antelope. A masochist.

He limped back through the Quarter and didn't think about purposes at all. Something had happened, though.

He had transformed again. His mind was no longer a soft cringing thing. It had become hard and able. The torment had lifted. Deeper into the Quarter the drums faded and he heard a string arrangement, like a distant whine *since you took it on the chin you've lost your toothpaste grin.*

He'd just been feeling sorry for himself. He needed to take the bull by the horns. Flip the alligator on its back, stare down the cheetah and the snake. He had been too much of a balladeer. Shy, coy, vulnerable. His whole goddamn life. But now he was about the Hard Blues. He realized that leaving town would be a kind of chickening-out. It would mean admitting that he couldn't handle New Orleans. Tantamount to saying you couldn't handle jazz. What kind of lie would such an admission prove his life to have been? The Bermuda triangle was dangerous, too, but it contained sunken galleons with Spanish gold—that was the point. *Fools rush in so here am I* he joined the jostling stream of tourists on Bourbon Street and tried to fit in *someone you adore it's a pleasure to be sad.*

He walked through the open door of a random tourist bar and ordered a drink. When he remembered that he'd forgotten to get money at the Amex office, he produced his plane-ticket and announced to the forty-something daytime-drunk tourists at the bar that it was for sale. The bartender said, "No soliciting, man," but made no move to stop it. Not a muscle. Didn't even take the cigarette out of his mouth.

There happened to be a fellow Chicagoan who'd already had enough. Maz said, "What's the matter, not glad to be unhappy anymore?" But the man didn't catch it. He'd already run out to a cash station. Maz sipped his drink and told the bartender he was opening a tab.

A few minutes later, the Chicago paisan returned and paid up cash for a quick way out. He wondered aloud if there was an AA chapter at the airport. When he saw the name on the ticket, he said, "Whoa, you got this from Maz Mazewski?" Then he said, "You didn't hurt him, did you?"

He seemed serious, but appearances had become untrustworthy. Maz replied that he *was* Maz Mazewski, and the man said, "Yeah, right, drink a few more for me," and darted out.

Now Maz had cash. He followed his banker's advice and drank a few more. The tourist bar was comforting. Could have been an airport bar. Maybe McWorld wasn't such a terrible destiny. Or maybe it was only tolerable if sparsely populated, like this place. The daytime crowd had faded away and the night people hadn't emerged from their caves yet. But nighttime approached, inexorably, and simple sleep wouldn't cure him, not now. He was all Hard Blues now. A railroad spike. He needed an orgy.

He asked the bartender if he knew where *Stagolee's* was and got handed a glossy brochure with sprawling neon cursive letters: "Hot Jazz!" A listing of jazz clubs with a punchy sentence following each name. He started to look for the place Leggit took him to, but remembered he never learned the name. Anyway, the map was too small to reach outside the high tourist district. The *Kove* wasn't even on there. He did locate the bar he found himself in now, though. He looked up and saw that, indeed, a combo was setting up on a little dais at the rear, under a neon sign that squealed *JAZZ!* In hot pink.

White boys, all of them. Looked like fifty-something college kids. Wore candy-striped vests with weak red bow-ties. Ice-cream vendors. He found *Stagolee's* on the map and set fire to the brochure and left it on the bar. The last thing he saw was the bartender's open mouth coming at him as he ducked out the door. He didn't leave a tip either. Fuck them all. The black ones and the white fakers. Fuck them all.

Stagolee's, on the other hand, seemed to be black-owned, or at least dedicated to giving that impression. Also, it was a more upscale kind of touristy, not on Bourbon but on Decatur. A converted warehouse. Thus port gave way to tourism as the leading industry. Honest labor replaced by shilling, milking the suckers. They had a micro-brewery on the premises. Maz ran into trouble right off the bat though, right at the front door, from a bull-necked football-player type bouncer. Yes, black, as all the staff seemed to be. He wore a dark suit and crimson tie with a white flower in the lapel. And a pork-pie hat. The guy shook his head and grinned smugly and said, "Dress code, man." When Maz pressed him he said, "Man, you sure you got enough money to drink here?"

Maz said he was a friend of Berta's. He gave his own name, too, but the doorman didn't recognize it.

"Friend a' Berta's huh?" He seemed afraid to look Maz in the eye. "What's her last name?"

"Bredaux."

"Yeah, like it says on the sign," he jerked his thumb to the

109

bill by the door. "What's she look like?"

Maz described her, and called her 'Dame' Berta this time.

The bouncer excused himself and picked up a phone behind a frosted glass partition. He stuck his head back around and said, "Mr. Mazooki?"

"Yeah."

He said OK and waved him in. He tried to apologize but Maz just barked, "Yeah, right" and brushed past him.

He wound his way through the little tables with their green candles and glanced at the red walls with their autographless autograph pictures of jazz greats. He only noticed Berta after she'd been standing in front of him for at least a minute. She wore another linen pants ensemble, this time a deep green, the color of moss under an inch or so of brown water. Strands of shells around her neck. She said, "You look like Billie Holiday in 1959."

"*Lady in Satin?*"

"Lady in a casket."

Maz crooned: "*You don't know what love is—*"

"C'mon Maz, sit down. Talk to me."

They took seats at the bar and Maz snapped his fingers and gestured the bartender over.

Berta said, "So, what, are you a finger-snapper now, too?"

"I'm just ordering a drink. People do it every day. Especially in your town."

"I think you should stick to getting high and lay off the booze for awhile."

"Berta. I'm so touched. No one's ever reached out to me

and cared. I'll never drink again."

Berta just looked at him. Looked in his face, aiming at his eyes, until he'd have to answer her stare. He refused to do it until he had a drink. He wanted to lay into her, really let her know what was up. She was so glib and easy about everything. He took a drink and turned to her and sang again: "*Until you've learned the meaning of the blues.*"

She said, "Seems like you're learning it."

"Bullshit. The Blues is just a music form. It's not some mystical hoodoo jooboo *experience.*" He rolled his eyes. Then he crossed them—it was a neat feeling.

"OK, I'll buy that, sure. Now to you: what has gotten into you, Maz? Did something happen in Chicago?"

"Nothing like that, like however you mean it, *happens* in Chicago. Chicago just grows, bigger and bigger, stronger and stronger. Your town, though—sinking into the mud and deserves it."

"Why don't you leave then?"

"Why does everybody want me to leave? 'Cause that's why I don't. I'm here and I've *been* here, so when are you people finally gonna just accept that and stop having such a big problem with it?" Maz' heart was racing. He tried to slow it down.

Berta touched him. He leaned into her embrace and drank it up. They squeezed each other. Maz tried to let the hug seep in. His muscles twitched, fighting a cringe, then began slowly to loosen. He almost cried, but he pulled himself away. He looked in her face—which *seemed* to show real concern—and tried to trust her.

But he couldn't. "Look, I guess it's just whatever, big party last night, getting old, whatever. Mid-life crisis. Y'know."

She ventured a smile. "I don't think I do."

"Hey, you just happened to be the unlucky friend to be sitting next to me for a little mood-swinging. Really, Berta, don't worry. Anyway, you're supposed to shut up and play the piano. Your fans, Berta," he tried a laugh, "think of your fans."

She nodded and kept her eyes on his face, maddeningly. She was prying, sending her invisible feelers deep inside him and poking under things.

"So can I sit in?"

She hesitated. Then, "Maz, of course. You're Maz Mazewski."

Maz's mind rang with a shout: *Don't feed me that self-deprecating shit, you know goddamn well you don't mean a word of it, you're laughing at me.* But he kept his feelings inside. Said nothing. Just nodded.

Then he got hit with a sudden inspiration. He'd make them laugh, since that's what he was to them. He'd do a burlesque number.

When Berta called him to the stage and he suggested "*Sheik of Araby*," she said, "Awww-right, fun!"

Maz surveyed the audience while Berta plunked out the opening chorus. The crowd was much bigger than what could ever fit in the *Kove*. Also different: it featured quite a number of well-dressed black patrons (mostly right up front). Many were obviously on dates, perhaps honeymoons, even, since a few had tourist brochures on the table in front of them. Berta spoke over her corn-pone kitschy bass and chords—spiked with major and minor seconds—to introduce her band and her guest the old-fashioned way. And when Maz' name came up the floor woke up in a vigorous round of real applause. They all smiled up at him and whispered in each others' ears. Then they went hazy beyond the lights. Maz saw them through a champagne lens, through bubbles. He suddenly wanted to wade out among them but he checked himself. He had to stay in control. He had to show them.

He began to do a ridiculous dance. He flopped his arms up like a cheap imitation of a bird and bent his knees slightly and jerked his feet up mechanically, like a tin-soldier marching. Then he did that Charleston thing with his hands on his knees and his knees scissoring and he opened his mouth and dropped his tongue down low and crossed his eyes. He heard some laughter. But only some.

I'm the Sheik, of Araby
All your love belongs to me ...

He sang it like a cross between Gomer Pyle (talking, not singing Jim Nabors) and Jimmy Durante. He did a trick he hadn't done since he was a kid: got his lower lip wrapped around his nose (for this he rolled his eyes upward, like he was trying to see something poised on his head).

At first Berta tried to get into it, throwing in outrageous tone-clusters and plodding out a stumbling, drunken bass-line. But then she just provided the standard changes like in a Vegas act. Like a blow-job for drugs. Maz noticed the waning interest from the piano but, like the resentful john, it only buoyed him. He jumped over the edge of the stage and landed with a splash among the tables. The people looked surprised, maybe even shocked, some of them. But amused. They traded glances with each other, trying to gauge what the appropriate response to these theatrics should be. He made an obscene sound with his mouth and grinned like a boy who'd just done a no-no. He barked out another verse on his knees, waving his arms heart outward, like misconceptualized swimming. He made intrusive eye contact with the well-dressed black ladies. Their dates chuckled. Maz was struck by a few pennies, coming first from one direction, then another. Folks were really laughing now, except for a handful who frowned and looked away— emphatically. Maz knew Berta would be one of these. Fuck her.

She wrapped it up abruptly with the old ladder-up-the-scale signal in the bass. Then she said into the mike, "Thank you, we'll just take a little break and be right back." She got up fast and stepped off the stage.

She didn't come to Maz, though, even though he stood there waiting for her. She walked right past him like she disdained to know him.

Maz followed her to the bar, where she tried too hard to sound pointedly nonchalant. "So how'd that number go?" he asked.

"It was a number," she huffed. "I didn't realize you were into physical comedy, Maz. I can see why the saxophone prob'ly started getting in the way."

"I'm branching out."

"Well, I see you've turned over a new leaf, but ... I don't like what's under it. Frankly, Maz," she turned to face him, "you're starting to give me the willies. I mean truly creep me out in a late-show, Sunday creature feature kinda way. I'm'on have to start calling you Morgus." She looked his face up and down and nodded her head, then shook it and looked away again. "But hey, whatever, I'm not out to save the world. Do your own thing, y'know. Not like you'd be the first to fall off the edge of a bottle or whatever it is you're on."

"Not out to save the world, huh? Yeah, like who is? Who the hell would be? I mean which *sucker* would be, huh?"

"Maz, what in heaven's hell are you doing?" She seemed almost to be crying, but, if so, they were angry tears, not sweet ones.

Some fan came by and praised Berta (trying to ignore Maz), saying her version of "What Is This Thing Called Love?" was "much appreciated." Maz thought what a nobody the fan must be: "much appreciated?" Stupid. Clueless. Berta smiled and said thank you. The adoring fan shrunk away.

Maz said, "Berta, I'm not really that ... I just ... well, I'm on vacation, doesn't a guy get to let his hair down and maybe ... do a few things he doesn't normally do?'

"Maz, that depends on *what* he does." Maz didn't know whether he was happy that he got a rise out of her, got noticed, or if it bothered him. He knew for sure that something was bothering him. He'd known that since Chicago. But that's exactly why it couldn't be this—Berta being teed at him. Too minor. He tried a conciliatory laugh but Berta didn't follow it through. She turned and started off. Maz stopped her by grabbing her sleeve. She turned and glared at him and Maz tried to figure out why in the world he felt so nervous. She unsettled him. Why? She had yesterday, too. Maz said, "Hey, tell me more about Leggit."

"I don't want to talk about him. Maz, I don't like him. He's a snake. I don't even like thinking about him." She touched her temples for emphasis. "Anyway, I've gotta play."

"We gonna do another one?"

This time she didn't hesitate: "I don't think so, Maz."

"Aw, c'mon, we'll do a completely different thing."

"Like?"

Was she seriously warming up or teasing him? "Like, uh, I was thinking something regional y'know, trad, like *'Lazy Bones'* or even ... *'Sleepytime Down South.'*"

"Whose trad is that?"

"Y'know," Maz grinned.

"Oh, yes, I do know. So you're gonna sing the *words* to those songs?"

"Sure, what I remember, make up the rest."

"How about *'Fat Little Feller wid His Mammy's Eyes'*?"

"Sure, I like that one."

"So, now I'm gonna do a minstrel show tune—"

"Oh shit, here we go—"

"No, here **you** go. I know you can't be serious, but it's a weak effort at humor, too." She perused his face again, as if genuinely searching. "And you're not smiling."

"Minstrelsy, minstrelsy, over and over again," Maz growled. "Maybe they're some nice tunes, maybe the music counts for something, you people are paranoid."

"Paranoid? Which people? You need a bleeding, Maz. You're feverish. Well …" she paused, reflected on some internal debate. "Yeah," she nodded, "I've got a scrip for you." Her voice had taken on a sharper, harder timbre. *You've changed … the sparkle in your eyes is gone.* But the flame in Berta's eyes was up a few notches. They shone, flashed, sent beams deep into him. Cold, though. She snatched up a cocktail napkin and tried to wave the bartender over to get a pen. Then she said, "Oh, this is better anyway," and produced a stick of lipstick from some fold in her garment and wrote on the napkin with that. She set it neatly on the bar between them, slid it toward him slightly, saying, "You want to find Leggit, or … this is where to go."

She flipped up the hand that had once held the napkin in a gesture of throwing something away, and shook her head in a fast deep shiver. Then she turned her eyes on him again. It was like there was something behind them, something like motion. A ripple like wind on water. Then she looked away and added, in a distant *sotto voce* snarl, "Good hunting."

Maz eyed the napkin. An address. He didn't know it. Where was she sending him?

"Hey, whoa …" It was all Maz could come up with. He felt like he had to tell her something, something like thanks but don't get overly dramatic about my business, I can handle my business, but her hand on his forearm hushed him. She changed again, but this time from cold to warm. Like going through seasons. She pressed his arm. Then his hand. "I guess you just need to work out some issues." She smiled, apparently in sympathy, not ridicule.

He looked back at the napkin, where already the lipstick was starting to bleed. When he looked up, Berta was already a few paces away. His audience with her was over.

Maz wondered why the lipstick on her mouth and the lipstick on the napkin seemed to be different colors, different shades.

She weaved back through the tables and the standing patrons parted to let her through and closed back up again, a body of dark shapes set against the soft bank of stage lights, until he couldn't tell anymore which shape was Berta.

Fuck it. He was up for action, not talk. Hard blue action.

1221 Marais.

What did she mean?

He had a vague sense where the address was. He walked out the door and in the general direction of his vague sense *take love easy, easy easy easy,* ready to flag a cab as soon as one came along.

One never came along. When he got to Rampart he despaired of the cab and approached a group of three men drinking out of brown paper bags in front of a red Lincoln, with a peeling vinyl top and an opera window. Black men.

He said, "One of y'all wanna give me a ride to this address here?" He held up the soggy red napkin, "I'm just not too sure where it is."

They all stared. First genuinely confused, then hammed-up confused. One of them finally said, "This look like a cab?"

Another one ribbed his friend, saying, "Naw, must be you look like a cab *driver*." The first one laughed out something about a dump truck driver ending in "Where you stay at."

Maz broke in: "Well, it's twenty bucks, and I know it's not far from here."

"Where?"

Maz made to hand the first man the napkin, but he jumped back and they all guffawed and the man shouted, "Man, get away from me wi' dat!" More laughter.

Maz laughed, too. It wasn't anything they said, it was the way comic verve came alive in their mouths in the speaking. As if obligated under some verbal contract among them to laugh this night and like it, the purpose was stamped on the way they said whatever it was they said. Such focused drive—just to be ridiculous. It was sound more than content. Infectious, though, an irresistible game.

Maz giggled out the address, "1221 Marais," and wondered if they wondered why he was laughing. But their laughter subsided into chuckles, then a slim trickle, then stopped.

It started again when one of them tapped his friend on the shoulder, as if in deep confidence, and said, "Do he know where he at?"

But when they finished up that round, the one who did most of the talking, the one who seemed to own the car, said,

"You got the twenty?"

Maz pulled it from his back pocket, careful to peel it from the wad in the pocket without pulling the wad out.

"OK. Let's take a ride." Low chortles all around.

The biggest ha-ha, the one that busted a gut on all of them (including Maz), came after they'd started the drive and the one who hadn't said anything yet, who'd taken a seat in the back with Maz, demanded shrilly that the car be stopped, got out and climbed in with the other two up front, hand over his face.

Maz asked for a hit off one of their bottles but they said: "Twenty dollars don't buy no refreshments!"

The drive only lasted maybe three blocks. Maz' destination seemed to be a source of special amusement. The driver said, "Awright it'll cost ya forty to git back." They would have laughed long at that one, but it was swallowed in the storm unleashed by the quiet one's observation—"Naw, he out here scoutin' f' black tail."

They dumped him off and Maz looked down at the sloping wet soft worn brick sidewalk. The typical herringbone pattern, with the typical weeds poking through at the seams. He knew he'd stood at this spot before. Or close to it. Hard to tell since so much of the city looked like it had been soaking and baking and falling off the bone since Storyville days.

In front of him was 1221 Marais. A large, weathered manse with front and side porches and balconies, set behind a grillwork gate. And a front yard with a dry fountain and a wild, crazy garden. French windows up top like eyes set at the wrong angle. The structure looked like it had been in the river for a century and was dredged from the bottom and placed here. A house of carved, planed, and adzed driftwood. Yet it also seemed to grow out of the soggy fuzzy brick foundation as naturally as the weedy banana trees that roosted all around the place like pigeons or roaches. There was a giant magnolia, too, and the noblest tree of the Southland, a live oak that sifted its brown flour softly, teasingly, through the soft moist fickle breeze. Always the breeze that gets you. Undoes you. He couldn't tell if it was cool or warm. Just, they were so wrapped up in each other: cool breeze wrapped in warm breeze enveloping a cool one hiding a warm one. Breezes *en brouchette*. Duplicity. Scented, too. Messages hidden in scents.

He opened the creaking gate and padded up the walk, up the porch stairs. The place was shuttered but Maz could see lights peeking through the windows, and he thought he heard murmuring voices—though the shifty wind made it impossible to tell the origins of sounds. The knocker on the door was a hand. He touched it first, as if asking permission. Then used it.

The door opened immediately and Maz saw a light-skinned black man in a spotless tux and a meticulously groomed handlebar moustache.

"Yes?"

"Um, Berta sent me."

The man looked annoyed. "Who?"

"Berta ... Bredaux."

"Sir, you must be a member or the guest of a member."

121

"How do you get to be a member?"

The doorman sized Maz up dismissively, then wrinkled up his face and said, "Membership is by invitation only and we are not soliciting new members at this time. Good evening, sir." He bowed his head slightly, looking at the ground, and shut the door in Maz' face.

Maz stood there on the porch, which, he noticed, seemed ready to fall through at any moment. The entire structure. It leaned. To the right. A marble would roll in a straight line from one side of the house to the other, easily. Ramshackle. Maz couldn't figure out how to fit the man in the tux and the house together in any logical way. He considered snooping around but a muffled sound—a slap?—from one of the windows scared him off. Exiting the gate, he heard either crying or laughing—pleading?—but he couldn't be sure which direction it came from.

He rounded the corner and recognized where he was. This couldn't be where Berta meant to send him. The bar from last night, only a lot quieter. No people spilled out the door onto the corner. No wonder he hadn't remembered the name. The place had no sign. It was just a low one story humble thing with a wide double door. Not even a beer logo in the little window, which had a shade pulled over it. The doors, though, stood open. So Maz walked in *walk right in*.

Empty. Almost. A bartender (different than before, a man) and two patrons. The jukebox played some dusty. One of the drinkers at the bar saw him come in and, after staring at him for a second, gently called to the bartender. The other drinker noticed him then, too, and all three of them stared at Maz.

The bartender said, "Uh, can I help you?"

"Yeah," Maz sidled up to the bar the way he'd seen Leggit do it and took a seat. "Uh, scotch and soda, I guess."

One of the patrons said, "Ain't got no band tonight."

Maz ignored it, pretended it wasn't obviously intended for him.

The bartender stood inert for a full second, then mixed the drink. It was scotch and seven-up, but Maz drank it anyway. The customer closest to him said, "Uh, you lookin' for somebody?"

The other guy mumbled, "He wanna be next door."

Maz said, "What, y'all never get white people in here?"

"Jus' ever' now and then," the bartender said, "when they got music." He chuckled. Raspy.

"I'm looking for Davis Leggit. He been around tonight?"

Silence. Then the bartender asked "Who?" and Maz repeated the name and got: "Naw, don't know that name." The drinker next to Maz shook his head and the other one nodded it.

The door to the back room opened. Yellow light spilled across the linoleum, then a gaunt shadow obstructed it. The shadow said, "Now, Clifford, why would you deny knowledge of me to a nice gentleman like this? Don't you know that Saint Peter almost lost his ticket to *paradiso* after denying his Lord three times?"

Leggit strolled over to Maz and placed his hand on his

123

shoulder, his arm stretched out at full length like he was grabbing at him from some hard-to-get-at place.

"This gentleman here happens to have contributed greatly to our culture. He is known by many as the 'Reverend' of jazz. Yet, as with so many who have contributed so much to the world, he feels as if not all is quite right at home. Is that a fair characterization, my Maz?"

Maz was truly not prepared for Leggit's verbal shenanigans. He said to the bartender, "Can I get another one of these?" and Leggit laughed and Maz noticed that he was wearing a long silk crimson robe over dark trousers and black shirt and dark, purplish tie.

Maz said, "I don't know ... Mister Leggit."

This got a laugh out of everyone in the bar and Maz was happy he finally scored one, without having to resort to silly faces.

"Were you hoping to hear some more o'that bad raunchy gutter scraping like you heard last night?"

"Oh, I was just making the rounds, y'know." Maz was at a loss. "Looking just for, y'know, whatever came up."

"Aahh—" Leggit brought hand to chin and closed his eyes, as if trying to remember something. The eyelids were darker than the rest of his face. A dark blue. "Antony come from Rome, come to seek his Cleo, uhhh?"

"I've been drinking no wine," Maz observed, "But Lord in Hell knows I've been seeing theater."

Leggit seemed amused. "Theater? Do you have a taste for theater? Theater is the genius of civilization. We'd just be gorillas without it."

Was that a note of conviction in the man's voice? Maybe there was hope for Leggit after all.

"So ... what's shaking?" Maz ventured, suddenly shy.

A low laugh, churlish. Then an intimate whisper, "Oh baby, dey's a whole lotta shakin' goin' on." Then he sighed and a look of terrifying boredom welled up in his eyes. Depthless exhaustion. The blue eyes went gray, flat, cement gray. But he bounced back just as quickly. "Well, the evening is young Maz, but I suspect a great part of it will soon be whiled away with tale-telling: the tale I hope you will honor me with, the tale of your life. Have you ever actually sat and rolled it all out for someone, someone as willing and eager as I to listen?"

But Maz was disturbed at the idea. Leggit made it sound like a confession. Also he didn't feel old enough to trudge through the past that way. So he said, "I'm not old enough to get away with boring people to death with memories."

"You're not as young as you were yesterday."

When was yesterday? "Nope," Maz said. "Neither are you."

"Come, Maz." He put his arm around Maz' shoulders, urged him gently off the barstool, and escorted him into the back room. Here he patted his robe-pockets and excused himself. Maz, left alone in the little room, not wanting to sit on the couch where his brain had been frozen and thawed out again the night before, noticed another door off to the side, ajar, lit by a soft a lamp. He peered in and saw a little office. No window. Desk, papers, envelopes. Pictures on the

125

wall in shadow above the arc of lamplight. Black and whites. Head shots. Leggit's favorite cats? Closer inspection revealed them all to be white men, of various different ages, different periods. He stood up against the wall on his toes and learned more: they were all the same man. At different stages of his life. They were all Jack Teagarden.

Leggit had returned, startling him. "Snoopin' around, huh?" There was a new sting in his voice, like a drunk suddenly and without warning goes from lubby-dubby to belligerent. But he went breezy again just as suddenly, with a forced laugh and a squeeze for Maz's shoulder. He sank onto the creaky desk chair and waved his hand at the pictures. Maz wondered when he would slide back into rage, or melancholy. He knew the type. Like Teagarden. Like Teagarden had turned on Maz at Monterey in '63. They had run into each other backstage. Jack T. was expansive, friendly, charming, until he huffed in Maz' ear: "You little fakin' shit, come up in here tryin' to play—bet you never even had the balls to lay a black gal." And ambled smiling onto the stage, into the lights, to applause because they loved him.

Leggit had ceased frowning and begun smiling. Wildly, with abandon. He showed his teeth and he rose out of his slump, to his full height. His dimples cut deeply, crevices, and the blue of his eyes went away, up above the arc of lamplight, and Maz saw only whites in his sockets, like boiled pigeon eggs.

"It's OK to snoop, Maz," he encouraged. "Explore." He tapped Maz on the nose with his forefinger, to underline his point. "Curiosity is a virtue, so much is clear." He pulled from a fold in his robe the elaborate snuff-box, waving it at Maz. "Won't you?"

Sweet-sweet. "Is that sweet-sweet?"

Leggit pursed his lips, then stretched them into a puckered smirk.

Maz took the snuff-box.

Leggit went to the wall and pointed out one of the photographs, "This is mah personal fave. You can see his fate written in the lines of his face. I wonder if he could? If he could even bear to look in the mirror." He turned to Maz, a tremor in his pointed finger, but Maz couldn't tell if the finger implicated him or Teagarden. "Monterey," Leggit gurgled. And they both said together: "1963."

Maz examined the snuff-box. The dim lamplight made it mysterious. It was an antique silver thing with an ivory inlay. Maz held it up close under the lamp. Scratched onto the ivory was an elephant spouting through his upheld trunk, and a palm tree.

Maz lifted it to his left nostril, rotated it open, and snorted. He repeated the action for his right nostril.

Cocaine. He'd done that before. Other stuff. He felt a heaving as if he'd been lifted off the ground by a stiff wind and knew it was heroin. They always told him H acted like an old friend, even if you'd never done it, you recognized it, felt like you knew it. There was something else though, something his body never met and his mind couldn't figure out.

Leggit's eyes were on him like a slate sidewalk looks up at

someone lying face down and a wave of searing heat swept over Maz' brain, a wind-whipped brush fire. He walked unevenly over to the couch in the other room—to get away from Teagarden—and let himself fall into it. His breathing didn't know which way to go—when out and when in. Another wave of flame came and this time left him in an arid barren space with wind (but no water). He heard Leggit say: "Dontchu fret, now, Maz. The rush will pass." Maz began babbling. He knew he was babbling—he recognized his own voice, but he couldn't keep track of what he was saying. Division Street came up a lot. Teagarden, too. His train trip down. Other train trips. Mississippi. LBJ. COFO. All the subjects he touched and left were like debris flying through the air in a tornado. But no rain. Yet. Eventually a light drizzle set in and cooled him down. Then the temperature was lovely—unearthly lovely or deep earthly underground in a cave. Warm. And a hard-on. The nasty couch he reclined on now he loved it, bit into it, into a yellow spot probably a semen stain. Leggit: "Come along Maz, I have just what the doctor ordered." "I don't feel like a drink." "How 'bout water?" "Yeah, water." Then Leggit's voice low, a growl, "How 'bout l'il black boy?" No. Maz wouldn't. Maz didn't answer. Not sure he heard right. Stood up and followed Leggit into the bar, drank a pint of water, splashed some on his face. Not the right water, though. Wanted river water. They left the bar and turned the corner. Maz walking just fine now, Maz just fine. They opened the gate to the old mansion and Maz said, "They won't let us in here." But Leggit said, modest hushed voice, "Oh, well. I'm a member." Slop, breeze up the porch. No, they were swishing. The same handlebar moustache, greeting Leggit, cordiality, then, "Oh, Mr. Mazewski. I'm so sorry, you should have told me." Everybody's sorry. Everybody will be sorry. *Till you've loved a love you've had to lose* Leggit said, "No matter. We'll be arranging something special for my dear friend. It's a special day, kind of a commemoration, so ..." and on and on *the music goes round and round then it comes out here* Maz couldn't believe how luxurious, plush, the place was on the inside. Turkish rugs worn leather easy chairs marble busts on mantles, broad, sweeping staircase with bunches of grapes carved out of wood becoming a banister, and at the foot of the stair, centered on a pedestal like a proud island, a black marble bearded head cut across with green veins. Parlors to the left and right. Leggit guided Maz right, where lounging grayish white men, in silk robes not quite as rich or dark as Leggit's, waiting, reading and sipping liquor. Black men in the other parlor? Wasn't sure anymore. Black and white swimming around in his head, his memory. Tangling. Then another, darker room, with rich shadowy oil portraits hung on the crimson velvety wallpaper. Here, beyond the candlelight, divans in the corners with people on them—in pairs—making quiet plans. Too dark to be raced, gendered, just shapes, possibilities, bubbles. Everyone red, really, but a soft red, burgundy, merlot, pinot noir. Everyone and everything the color of wine *is fine*. A dark paneled hall with creaky floor, small etchings in plain frames, of satyrs, nymphs, a god rising out of the water with horns. "Wait"— his own voice, pausing to look through a slightly ajar door—onto a kitchen. A brightly lit fully functional 1950s-looking Formica kitchen. The walls bright yellow, lemon meringue. Appliances enamel and chrome. They had a woman, a real woman, standing at the stove, slim, fortyish, in a Doris Day starched dress and stiff meticulously styled honey hair. Somebody's white housewife. At the table sat a young black man in gangsta get-up—bandanna under cap, Chicago Bulls jersey gold rope chains gold teeth. In a darkened red corner more men in suits, a spectating woman, too, fortyish, elegant, pearls. The homey suddenly started from the table the homemaker gasped. But the scene vanished, washed away by the tantalizing torturous water-flecked breeze of Leggit dragging him by the sleeve *but not for me*. Leggit walked him down a narrow airless back staircase, said, "That boy did you wrong las' night, didn't he?" "What? Who?" "That little uppity one with the cornet. Thinks 'cause he can play a horn he can look at you that way. Disrespect you that way." "I'm used to that. I mean what does a guy have to do? How much of a guy's life does he have to give to get respect from ... them. Some of them." "Tell me this Maz," stepping out into an enclosed patio with ferns in giant jugs and vines, Passion Vines with science-fiction blooms *fly me to the moon* creepers, elephant ears, "Ever known somebody to not respect you right when your dick's shovin' deep inside 'em? Huh? Like that? Huh?" and the motion to go with the ocean, fitful jerks of his wiry pelvis "Bitch! Yeah! Huh? Like that, my man?" No. Not. "Not that I know of." "Good answer!" Laughing, again, laughing all the time, at what?

"Long as what you don't know don't hurtcha. Just gotta make a fast getaway sometimes, am I right?" A dim light through a garage, no, stable, at the end of the old kitchen and slave-quarter, all, all of it all opened up to the patio. Inside, outside all inside-out. They made for the light, the restless golden haze. The light gaslight. Leggit said, low, for effect, for show, since it could be for no practical purpose where they found themselves *if the moon turns green and shadows get up and walk around, clouds come tumbling to the ground* "Now I wantcha to know, the one we got for you, he's definitely a virgin, now." In the stable. Dirt floor. Stalls with real mules. Kerosene lantern. But the only human thing Maz saw was a thirtyish or so very large muscular very black man in overalls with no shirt, Leggit approaching him. "Where's the boy, Abner?" "Please, sir, not mah boy," wringing his hands looking at the ground, Leggit struck him in the face. "What the hell's wrong witchu, boy?" Maz flinched, like the next blow coming for him, him taking his punishment and what was he doing here he shouldn't be here but *that old black magic you weave so well.* All a game, anyway, nasty game. Man being paid. Abner? Ridiculous. Play-acting, a game. "No suh, please suh, no." "Mah friend here's come a long way, from way, way up north, to get a little boyhole ... You want we should fuck you instead?" Big bad black man crying. Crocodile tears. A boy stepping out of one of the stalls and into the lantern light. Just a boy. Not a cheetah. Darker. Smaller, slighter, unmagnificent, unblessed. Skin not Terracotta. Mud. Black mud. The lips a slightly darker shade, like his, the other one's, like lipsticked *lips are lovely but the wrong lips*

131

but it's alright with me. Black eyes, boat-shaped, banana bugs *they'll sparkle they'll bubble* walked out slowly and stood there right in front of Maz waiting. Not a cat. Just a boy. He wouldn't. But he would. Fuck them all. The just-a-boy shifted to another foot, a little sideways, and Maz saw the high rounded bubble of his ass, in rough wool knee-pants tied with a rope. What to do? *We kissed in a field of white and* flicker of lamplight and mule breath and man-breathing a hot stifling place Maz ripped his own shirt *and stars fell on Alabama* and Leggit whispered into the boy's ear (softly kneading his shoulder) and the boy winced and grimaced, mean, and marched over to Maz and said, "Man, fuck you, witcho white-ass goofy self," and spat at his feet *except when soft rains fall I've forgotten you like I should except* Maz, voice cracking, bad singing: "Oh yeah? OK, c'mere," pulling the kid to himself roughly by the arm. Kiss the boy, punk *you don't know how lips hurt until* all over his face, licked him, boy kept dodging his mouth *kissed and paid the cost* and trying to keep his own lips clamped shut *that have tasted tears* so Maz forced the boy to his knees and unzipped his own pants and there his dick was bigger than he'd ever remembered seeing it he rubbed it on the boy's warm soft (dry) brick face, mudbrick, but he kept jerking around and not cooperating. Leggit, in a quiet stern voice: "Now cut that crap out and suck the man's dick like I told you." The boy harrumphing like, just like *in love's smoldering ember one spark may remain* and Leggit saying, "OK, that's it, excuse me Maz, I'm sorry about this." For show, Leggit the showman, he jerked the boy up by his arm and dragged him over to a crate and tripped him up and bent him over it and with his foot on the small of the boy's back, he removed his belt and Maz looked at the large older big bad black one who looked bored until he saw Maz looking, then contorted his face in rote portrayal of fear, hate everything that comes so easily, all of it too easy, eternally rehearsed, too smooth *sipping champagne with a frown* Leggit had the boy's pants down. His buns rose and crested like a wave of soft clay, polished smooth, downy like raw silk, a soft pillow for a rough face, treated with oils and lotions for a full year before this moment and then the belt came down and the kid whimpered and shivered. Gaslight flicker and ropes and tack and in between the snapping of the belt *from the way I feel when that bell starts to peal* and the boy's noises the night air consisted of a drone of amphibians and water insects and it had sweet olive and it had exhaust too, like both things, and the human things, had to breathe, on Maz, on this. Countenanced. Leggit finished the fifth stroke and *moving shadows like the oldest magic word* let the boy up and pushed him and he obediently sucked the dick—in its place fetid and musty as the mildew on the walls of the barn over the past three days of no washing. Maz had regressed, he was a barbarous ancestor *how strange the change from major to minor* the kid just bobbed his head back and forth mechanically, getting wet only the top two inches so Maz lifted him up to his feet and led him back to the crate and bent the boy and kneeled him over it and Maz' face glancing the surface of the brown swell of ass (but it didn't refresh, didn't cool) and Maz stood planted bent-kneed stable and pushed in, in like warm alluvial richness, and the boy's noises like the origin of song and Maz saw rivers and flat roads brown or red or rust and tangled green carpet, snakes, black branches of wet oaks and bricks returning to clay in the mud he pushed, deeper, deeper, the crate splintered and collapsed and Maz dove deep down where the sun and heat couldn't get through, the bottom of the river rolling with the force of its main current, the main vein, the groove, and then the current stopped and he was out again, in air.

He fell on the shore and rolled over.

Leggit was talking. "Now go ahead, git your pants, now ... Uh-huh. Now get on back to the house. Talk to DeeDee ... Roger, you take him. Awright."

Roger—the boy's dad in the movie—patted the boy on the back and said, "You awright."

Maz craned to see. The boy turned slightly as he hurried out and Maz caught one last profile. Grinning. Not broadly but…definitely. As if he'd accomplished something and felt entitled to a pat on the back. What had he accomplished?

Maz lay there and looked up, at the webbed and rotting wooden beams above him. The water was winning. But it didn't cool. A rawhide whip hung on a nail on one of the mule stalls. Hot, wet scent of manure. He cleared his throat—phlegm in it. He felt like a discarded tire. He said, "So why didn't you use the whip on him?"

"Maz, what do you take me to be?" Leggit struck a match. Lit a cigar, a panatela. "Whips are for field niggers. The belt is standard procedure for domestics."

The self-satisfied grin on Leggit's face made Maz nauseous, but he managed to sit up, stand up, zip up. He said, "What kind of a thing are you, Leggit?"

"Well, well," Leggit laughed—as a rhetorical gesture, Maz guessed. "What kind of thing am I?" He gripped the lapels of his robe and bent his head and paced in mock thought. Had to be the only kind of thought he did, anymore, under his shock of blue hair. He gazed at Maz' face, pointed his cigar at him, blew smoke, and said, "Honest man." He narrowed his eyes at him. "That's what kind of thing I am."

Bullshit. Anyway, Maz would never be able to fathom Leggit. It just wasn't in him. He was just not close enough and not far enough away. Or something. He felt bad. He couldn't help it. He felt bad. He felt like he had done something wrong. Somehow Leggit could go through life not feeling that way. Maz asked him, "So why didn't you fuck him?"

"Ooh," he chortled. "I prefer the little girls."

Of course. "So the police in this town let this kind of thing happen."

"Many of them are members."

"What about the black ones?"

"Sure, many of them are members, too. We don't discriminate. 'Cept in taste matters, as I'm sure you as an artist with high standards can appreciate."

"What do the black members do?"

"Well, most times they head up to the second floor."

"What's up there? Shackles? A stockade?"

"Nooo," he fluttered his eyelashes, "That's where we keep

the little white boys and girls. Oh yeah, me and a black buddy a'mine one time, I got done up in blackface y'know, and we went up there and raped us a coupla white girls in their pink little girl beds."

Maz pushed out onto the patio, in search of something breathable. Leggit gurgled on behind him. "That was… Heather? I believe…and Mandy. Fine girls. Unfortunately, they do get older. But then that's just a different bottle a' wine, I suppose."

Maz wanted to get away. He wanted to stride, briskly, but all he could manage was a dazed meandering. Leggit followed him, right on his heels, mumbling on about twilit memories.

The patio looked different than before, looked commonplace. He liked it better when he could still believe it contained secrets.

He heard music. A trad jazz ensemble. Not the new sounds. Old style. Dixieland. How fresh. Maz wanted it, suddenly and desperately. He fumbled his way toward the sounds, along the wall of the slave quarter attached to the barn. The music came from behind a high stand of bamboo. He wanted to make a bee-line to it, but the plants were impenetrable, so he followed the bamboo until it ceased. Leggit stumbled after, from the tone of his voice in smiley land again. "Maz? Maaazz? Where are you going?" Giggling.

Maz found an open chain-link fence leading to another patio—more dark brick, another slave quarter, this one apparently in the midst of renovation. These patios were everywhere. How could there be so many? How did they fit them all into the same square bounded by four streets? To leave the sidewalk was to begin a descent. Maz' consolation was the thought that it would all be under the Gulf one day. Good. It needed to go. Below the surface of memory.

The music wasn't on this patio either—it was still one more removed. Through an iron gate in the opposite wall. A pool party.

Pushing at the gate, he found it was unlatched. The pool had a Sevillian tile border and lights beneath the surface. People lounged around on iron furniture in what looked like togas. White combed cotton robes, actually. Club robes. Each bore the same logo on the breast pocket. A dark bearded head. There was a little cabana bar, a cocktail waiter with a tray. And sex. This time heterosexual, and all apparently adults. Isolated, discreet pairs, in shadows. Polite sex. But Maz was most interested in the bandstand. He'd come to drink the old-time sounds—the old-time white dance band sounds.

They were OK. They were good. Doing a Dixieland retro arrangement of "What A Wonderful World." They wore white shirts, ties, dark pants. But their faces. Yep, it was make-up. Minstrel make-up. Blackface. You could see authentic skin-color on their necks. They were a mixed band, actually. Racially speaking, that is. Their real races. Their necks and hands were black, white, pink, yellow, and brown. But their faces were all the same: shiny, gaudy, unreal black. Pure surfaces, hollow types, to be filled by whomever.

Maz didn't feel like a swim after all, not in the music or the pool. He'd never get close to that music, either. He didn't even want to. The sounds just gasped on like some cyborg that had forgotten how to be sentient. It didn't interest him anymore. Was it him or the music that had changed? *Your smile a careless yawn* he felt Leggit's amphibious paw on his shoulder.

"Hol' on Maz, what are you in such a hurry for? You can't get out of here without me anyway."

Maz wanted to sink to the ground. He wanted more than anything just to lie on the damp mossy brick. He remained standing but he closed his eyes. Colors swam around behind his eyelids. He waited for a clarifying breeze. It didn't come. Leggit looped an arm through his and escorted him back through the layers of brick, foliage, gates. Took him along the side of the big house, as if Maz were no longer presentable enough to be allowed inside. Maz agreed, he wasn't. He was a lower organism. But isn't that what he wanted? That was the whole kicker about wanting things: what you want is what hurts you.

Leggit said, "I bet you figure you'll be gettin' back to Chicago now huh?"

Of course. Everyone knew it. He had to leave here, anyway. He was just made of the wrong stuff. "That's what I figure," he said.

Maz wanted to turn his ears off. Because things whispered at him. The boards of the house, the windowpanes from behind their shutters, the creaking empty porch. Even the aged downy brick walkway registered him, with an unlikely scraping sound. Leggit called after him from the steps, after gently shoving him through the gate, "Well, maybe we'll see ya, yet, now. You'll prob'ly wanna pay a visit again. Awright, take care ... be careful on these streets ..."

He kept talking. Maz didn't know when the Leggit on the porch stopped and when the one in his head took over, a tongue in his ear.

There was a film of moisture on the bumpy undulating sidewalk that made walking difficult. Maz realized he was barefoot. The slugs had come out, leaving silvery veins shining and making the walk even more slippery, and placing their boneless bodies under his feet in kamikaze efforts to trip him up. More indistinctness, more blurriness, more touching something isn't really touching it, playing something isn't really playing it. Maz tried to picture the Sears Tower rising up on the shoulders of a hundred years of skyscrapers, all in a legible grid, cool and confident, sighted and framed by Milwaukee Avenue honing in on a perfect diagonal across miles of tended city. But the sight flickered and wavered, because he was crying.

It became a human form instead, a darting human form with malicious intent. And then another. Appearing and vanishing, leaving echoes in the air. The night was hazy. Slithering shapes. Natives, he guessed. Were they clearing a path for him or stalking him? Human cheetahs, man their only predator. One suddenly brushed against him. It said "Excuse." Maz kept stumbling forward, not knowing where. He felt like a severed head that keeps growing hair. His body's movement was purely a routine biological matter, had nothing to do with himself. But then volition came to him, desperately, and he stopped and turned. A shape was indelibly there. Just stood there returning his gaze. Maz made no move to walk or speak. He just stood and beheld the boy, until others appeared behind him. On the same snaking sidewalk as the afternoon before. Skin like the backside of a magnolia leaf, soaked too long in a mosquito puddle. The eyes flat, black, no reflection. The others, too, were all boys. Just boys. Not cheetahs. Not snakes either. Nothing magic. Nothing unusual. Just boys. The haze lifted. When the arm furled out, it contained not a cornet, but its cousin, the handgun *why not take all of me.*

Maz felt calm, cool. But angry. Victim to victim. They'd been toying with him his whole life and Maz's Mister Niceguy approach had only made them disrespect him. They needed some sage counsel from what DuBois called the "stronger and wiser group," even if it was the last thing one strong wise crazy asshole ever said. "You people, I can't believe y'all."

"Whut?"

"They got a word for people like y'all who just mooch off society and don't produce anything and can't be serious and can't be responsible and handle your fucking shit."

Maz was right up in his face, nose to nose with the gunman, but not blustering. He played it smooth, soft. He was changed again—for good, this time. He had busted out of his dusty, dank cocoon, a multi-colored winged thing.

They grabbed him and pushed him against a tree. They held him and the one with the gun looked almost not angry. He had a flash in his eyes that bordered on amusement.

"Shee," he spat. "Can't you see what I got in my hand here, man?"

Maz stepped back, collected himself. He needed the right words. He figured he could hit the right groove if he could just start bopping and fly away.

"My niggers," he muttered, trying to get off the ground, "ma niggas …"

Someone behind him tripped him up and knocked him to his knees.

"*You've taken the best*," Maz sang, "*so why not take the rest?*"

The gun, so familiar, rose again to greet him.

His horn a rootin'-tootin' they shot him execution-style on the corner of Basin and Rampart. His body toppled neatly and lay there, on a spot of sidewalk where the concrete had cracked from weather, revealing the older layer of brick underneath. Maz' pool touched both. Even after the cool rain came down and mixed it all up.

Berta Bredaux read the police reports in the morning paper but there was nothing—about Maz. She was heartened, but not convinced. The man at the *Dauphine Courtyard* said he hadn't returned last night, or in the morning, yet. Sure enough, the "unidentified middle-aged white male" made the evening report. She went down and ID'd him—a disgusting, horrible business that she meant to have a word with Maz about when they next met. She arranged to have the body sent back to his Sweet Home. Chicago received the news the same day, shocked and respectful. Appropriate.

That night Berta sang in public for the first time since the early sixties. She dedicated the tune to Maz. Did "*But Beautiful*," did it like Billie.
Love is funny
Or it's sad
A good thing
Or it's bad
But ...
—as sung by Billie Holiday, February 19th, 1958, for *Lady in Satin*.

C. W. Cannon writes fiction and non-fiction. He is the author of three previous novels: *Soul Resin, Katrina Means Cleansing*, and *French Quarter Beautification Project*. His writing is found most frequently in *The Lens* (thelensnola.org), where he contributes essays on New Orleans culture, the South, and race. He teaches writing and New Orleans Studies at Loyola University New Orleans.